Saltwater Secrets

ANJ
Press

Pittsburgh

SALTWATER SECRETS

ANJ Press, First edition. June 2020.

Copyright © 2020 Amelia Addler.

Written by Amelia Addler.

Cover design by Charmaine Ross at CharmaineRoss.com

Maps by Nate Taylor at IllustratorNate.com

For the whisper that drowns out self-doubt

Recap and Introduction to *Saltwater Secrets*

Welcome to the third installment of the Westcott Bay Series! In book one, our heroine Margie Clifton moved to San Juan Island to start her events business at Saltwater Cove. She also hoped to make a second home for her three kids Tiffany, Jade and Connor following her divorce.

Margie's life was turned upside down when she discovered that her ex-husband Jeff spent decades hiding a secret child, Morgan Allen, from an affair with the late Kelly Allen. With the help of Chief Hank, Margie was able to piece her life back together and reunite her family – including the new addition of Morgan. Margie also started an exciting new chapter in her life when Hank proposed!

In book two of the series, Morgan moved to San Juan Island, excited to live with Jade and to start her new photography business. She was also keen on learning more about the woman caught on a grainy surveillance video – a video that clearly showed the car that struck and killed her mom. Despite the best efforts from the sheriff's department, however, the case went cold.

That was, until, the handsome and charming, if not too irksome Luke Pierce walked into Morgan's life. He first annoyed her as the videographer to accompany her new business, and he *then* had the gall to ask her out. Their strong personalities clashed, and Luke had no choice but to leave both Morgan and the island for good.

Before he managed to escape, Luke ran into his Uncle Brock and Brock's not-so-innocent girlfriend, Andrea. With some charm and help from the sheriff's department, Luke captured Andrea's confession and she was arrested for the hit-and-run of Kelly Allen.

Morgan and Luke reunited, as did Margie and Hank (whose wedding was *almost* called off due to the protests of Hank's daughter Amanda) and it seemed that everyone would get to have a moment's peace.

In book three, Jade sets her mind to getting a fresh start after her divorce from Brandon is finalized. But her plans are thrown into chaos when a string of bizarre crimes seem to follow her around the island. Jade is determined to keep a positive attitude – especially because she gets to spend more time with Matthew. Unfortunately, Matthew's life is torn in two when someone from his past appears on San Juan...

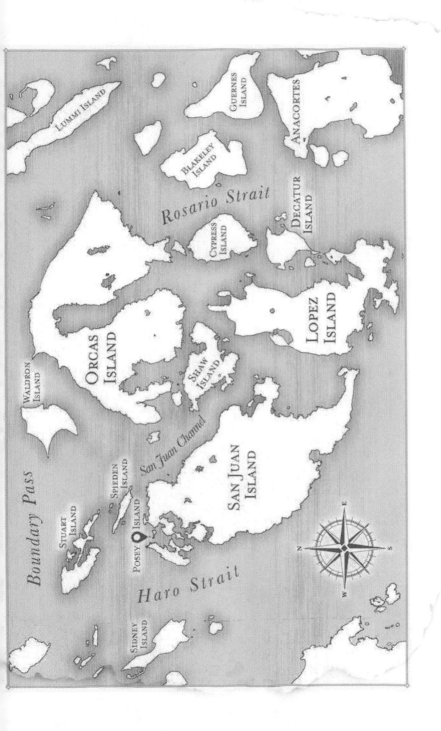

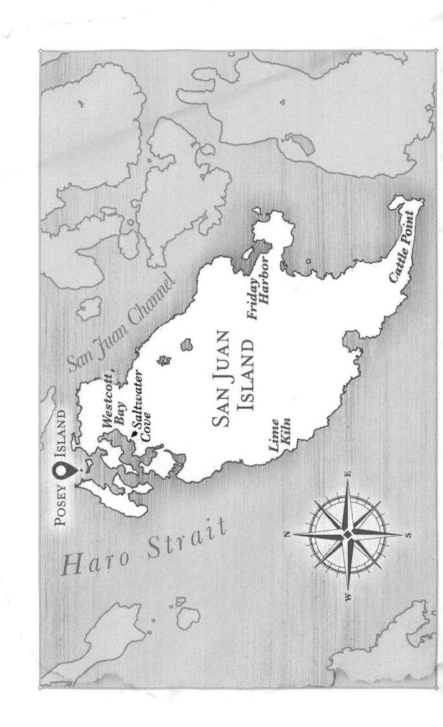

Chapter 1

When Jade first got the suggestion of celebrating Valentine's Day by herself, she thought it was *beyond* embarrassing.

"Doesn't that seem a bit...self-absorbed?" she asked her counselor Greta.

Greta smiled. "Well – no. It doesn't have to be that way. It's an alternative way to celebrate the holiday for people who don't have a romantic partner. You celebrate yourself and you can be your *own* special someone."

Jade had to stop herself from visibly cringing. Wasn't it enough that she was willing to give this whole counseling thing a chance? Did she really have to sign up for the entire package – like agreeing to be her "own special someone?"

On the other hand, counseling *had* been quite helpful over the past few months. Greta guided her through a lot of shame surrounding the divorce, and helped Jade find strength that she didn't know she had.

Even so. This was too much.

Greta leaned in. "What are you thinking Jade?"

"I just..." She cleared her throat; there was no need to hurt the poor woman's feelings. "I don't think that's something for me."

"Okay," Greta said with a nod. "I can understand that. But would you agree that you have a lot to celebrate from this past year? Do you feel proud of yourself?"

Jade sighed. "I guess."

"Are you proud of yourself for that progress? For putting yourself out there?"

"Yes, but..."

Greta sat there, eyes fixed, but saying nothing.

Ugh. Jade didn't feel as jumbled about everything as she did months ago, but she still didn't feel quite right, either. She didn't feel...the way everyone else *looked*. Other people looked put together. They looked like they were happy. Calm, even.

"But what?" Greta prompted.

"It's just..." Jade paused. "There's still a lot of work to do."

Greta folded her hands in her lap. "Of course. You've identified this before, Jade, that you are the kind of person who always wants to improve. But just because you see room for improvement, it doesn't mean that you should despair."

"Right. That's a good point."

"So if you did Valentine's Day the 'Jade Way,' what would you do?"

Jade suddenly had an undeniable itch on her nose. Why did she always feel so fidgety when she was there? "Well. I wouldn't say that I was celebrating myself. But I could celebrate – maybe a little – the progress I've made in the last year. And I could set goals for the coming year?"

"That does sound a bit more like you, doesn't it?"

"Yes," Jade said with a smile. "I think so."

Jade debated what she'd actually have to do to make an honest effort. Her first thought was to have a bowl of ice cream and stick a candle into it, but the image of that was too sad to actually carry out.

Instead, she got the idea of going on a hike and having a little picnic. It seemed much less pathetic than a sad, solitary candle; on Valentine's weekend, she drove to Lime Kiln Park and set out on a quiet trail.

It was a great idea...at first.

To start out, she wandered along several paths before finally reaching her destination – the top of a rocky hill that over-looked the ocean.

Jade never grew tired of views like this. From high above, she could barely hear the sounds of the water, with the boats slowly bumbling along, and the waves crashing into the rocks at the shoreline. She loved looking out and seeing the sea stretch to other little islands, dotted with green trees and rolling with mountains. It felt like she could see forever.

She was still close enough to the water that she'd be able to make out an orca, but that was an unlikely sight today – it'd be months before the residents returned to San Juan. There was still plenty to admire, though, and for a moment, the beauty of the ocean made her feel whole again.

As she took it all in, a breeze blew through her jacket and caused a chill to run down her back – she'd gotten quite warm walking up the hill, but now the wind cut into her.

She was glad that it was cold, though; there was hardly anyone else at the park that day to witness her being her "own special someone."

Jade closed her eyes and enjoyed the solitude. She didn't mind being alone. She didn't even mind being alone for Valentine's Day. It was easier than being with her ex-husband Brandon for any holiday, actually, because she used to hope that he might do something sweet or nice.

Or worse – she would plan dinner, or get a gift for him, and it was always wrong in some way. Either she'd spent too much on his gift, or too little. And the meal she planned was too early, or too greasy and it made him feel sick – and, he'd add, *she* didn't need the extra calories.

Jade turned to find a place to settle down for her picnic. She still thought that counseling was odd at times. It made her say things that she was embarrassed to admit, and it also made her do things she didn't always feel comfortable doing. It wasn't just weird assignments like going on this hike, but also in practicing different thinking patterns – patterns that didn't echo her ex-husband's critical comments.

Counseling was the reason that she no longer thought it was one of her own personal faults to expect her partner to buy a card, or even attempt to be pleasant on Valentine's Day. She now realized that for all those years, she felt too frivolous and silly to actually expect something – anything, even a single flower – for her birthday.

Now she was confident – well, as confident as she could be about anything – that it was okay to have standards. It didn't make her shallow or selfish. It meant that she was standing up for herself. Like Greta always said – you teach people how to treat you. And Jade was ashamed by how badly she had allowed Brandon to treat her.

Jade finally found a flat spot under a large madrona tree and spread out the small blanket she'd packed. Carefully, she pulled out a slice of the chocolate cake that her mom had made for Valentine's Day.

It had just appeared on her doorstep with a note that said, "I love you!"

It was one of the nicest things she'd ever gotten for Valentine's Day. That was another thing – looking back on the last few years of her relationship with Brandon, she was exceedingly embarrassed. What did people think of her when they saw her putting up with his behavior?

Jade shook her head. Greta always reminded her that it was impossible to change the past and she knew that there was no use dwelling on it...

She unwrapped the cake and pulled a fork from her backpack. Yes, it was hard to believe that she had put up with Brandon's increasingly bad behavior. He wasn't always that way, though – it took years for him to get *that* bad. She didn't know how it happened at all, though. She was still trying to understand her role in it.

Jade took a bite of cake and reached out to touch the red bark of the tree next to her. It was a gorgeous, grizzled thing. How it grew at the top of this hill through strong winds was beyond her. She leaned back and admired the waxy green leaves, holding firmly in the cold winter breeze. She pulled out her cell phone and snapped a picture of the scene to remember the moment.

She was looking at the picture when she heard something snap behind her. Jade whipped around, scanning the trees and rocks for anything that looked like, say, a happy couple out on a hike, but there was no one there. Maybe it was just a bird. Or maybe...

Maybe it wasn't such a great thing that there weren't a lot of people in the park? What if there was just *one* other person, someone whose plans weren't as wholesome as hers?

She quickly finished the rest of the cake, feeling guilty that she wasn't savoring her mom's baking as much as it deserved. Her mom would understand, though.

Jade quickly packed up her blanket and took another look around. She tried to make it look casual, so if someone *was* watching her, they wouldn't know that she was on to them. Or that she was crazy. She took one last look around before heading down the trail.

After a few minutes, she felt confident that no one was following her. It was just her overactive imagination. Even so, she decided that it would be just as well for her to celebrate her progress and set goals as she took a shorter trail back to the parking lot.

For the things she was proud of...well, she liked to think of things she was thankful for. Jade knew that she had a wonderful family who supported her through the divorce. She also got to live with her best friend Morgan, who was always a source of support and entertainment.

Outside of that, Jade seemed to be well liked at her job and was even allowed to work from home full-time now – her boss really trusted her for some reason. And Jade was starting to branch out – she started getting involved in activities on the island, like the county council.

As far as goals...well, she wanted to do something for the people of San Juan Island. There was a new project that she learned about through the council meetings. And despite all of the jokes that she kept hearing at her mom's now famous Sunday dinners, she was *not* going to meetings to pick up a boyfriend. Far from it. She truly wanted to find a way to do her part as an islander.

Not that there was anything wrong with wanting to have a boyfriend. But there also wasn't anything wrong with *not* having a boyfriend.

In fact, she wasn't ready for a boyfriend. Not until she understood herself better and could be sure that she wouldn't fall into the same sort of dysfunction that she had with Brandon.

This wasn't on Greta's advice, but rather something that she felt deep in her heart. Just because she found someone interesting, smart, insightful, and even handsome...it didn't mean he'd make a good boyfriend.

No, even someone seemingly as decent as, say, Matthew couldn't be trusted. Sure, he was nice enough when he came to Sunday dinners or when he helped with Morgan's mom's case, but who knew what he was *really* like?

Brandon was nice at first, too. Almost *too* nice; he tried so hard to impress her and her family. Jade wasn't the only one who fell for it.

She paused for a moment and pretended to tie her shoe; there were no other sounds or movements. Good. It was all imagined – or perhaps a bird or something.

She kept walking, a bit slower now. This was the year to work on herself, not the year to rush and find her "special someone." Maybe she would never date again. And maybe she would never get married again – it might just be better that way. It was too soon to say – and too soon to worry about.

When she got back to the parking lot, it was already starting to get dark. Her car was the only one in the lot. She was busy digging in her backpack to find her keys when she walked up to her car and heard a crunch under her feet.

Confused, Jade looked down to see what she was stepping on. It looked like...glass?

She pulled out her cell phone to use as a flashlight. "Oh my gosh!"

The driver's side window of her car was broken, bits of glass shattered onto the ground and blanketing the driver's seat.

Her heart rate picked up. She turned around to make sure that no one was approaching her; it seemed like she was the only one there, but she didn't feel quite secure in that belief anymore.

Jade leaned in to look at her car. She didn't know how she would clear the glass so that she could sit down. The nearest person that could help her was...

Jade sighed and dialed her mom's number.

She answered right away. "Hi sweetie, happy Valentine's Day!"

"Hey Mom – do you have a second? I'm at Lime Kiln Park and I just got back to my car, and...my window is broken."

"What! Are you okay?"

"I'm fine, I'm just not sure how to clean it up. I thought maybe, if you're not busy, you could stop by and – "

"Yes, I'll come right now! Oh, wait a second..."

Jade heard some murmuring in the background as her mom conversed with Hank.

There still didn't seem to be anyone else in the parking lot. Not that she knew what she would do if there *was* someone – would she run? Where? And how far could she make it?

"Okay honey, just hang on a second. Hank is sending one of the deputies over, he should be there soon."

Jade felt her stomach drop. "No, that's okay, I'll just sweep it out and – "

"Don't be ridiculous! They're already out on patrol. Oh, hang on a second."

More murmuring.

"Oh good, it looks like Matthew is only a minute away."

Jade shut her eyes. She'd mostly succeeded in avoiding Matthew for the past few months, outside of Sunday dinners. There was no need for her to spend time with someone...well, like him. Maybe she could try running? How far could she get? Morgan would surely come pick her up.

"Honey? Are you still there?"

"Yes, I'm still here," Jade replied with a sigh. "It's fine, please don't worry, I think I'll just go home."

"Just hang on! I don't want you cutting yourself on the glass. Stay on the line until he gets there, okay?"

"Sure."

Jade looked up just as a patrol car pulled into the parking lot.

Chapter 2

It was just before six when Matthew heard a call over the radio about a vehicle prowl in the Lime Kiln parking lot. He was glad to respond – it was almost the end of his shift and nothing interesting happened the entire day.

He turned his car around just as his cell phone rang. It was Chief Hank.

"Hey Chief."

"Hey, are you headed to Lime Kiln?"

"Yeah, what's up?"

"Good." Chief cleared his throat. "It's Jade – someone busted her car window."

Oh. That made it even more interesting. Not that he was happy her car was vandalized, but...

"I'm on it." Matthew said, stepping on the gas. "I'll be there in a minute."

"Thanks. I'll tell Margie."

Within seconds, Matthew turned onto Lighthouse Road; he had to remind himself to slow down as he approached the parking lot. It got dark so quickly in the winter that by this hour, he could only see a few feet ahead. Luckily, Jade was easy to spot – she was the only one there as his headlights swung around the corner. She raised a hand and gave a small wave.

Matthew felt his chest tighten. She must've been standing there in the complete darkness by herself. Or was she...with someone? It was Valentine's Day.

"Hey there," he said as he got out of his patrol car.

She smiled. "Hey. Sorry. I called my mom and before I knew what was happening, dispatch was already involved."

No, she definitely wasn't with anyone else – she must've gone into the park on her own. Or had she come with someone who then left her to fend for herself?

"Don't be sorry," he replied, putting up a hand. "I was happy to stop by. It's been a very boring night."

"Well – thank you, I appreciate it. I don't think this is really all that interesting, though – just a lot of broken glass. I'm not really sure what to do, but I need to find a way to clean it all up."

Matthew shined his flashlight into the car and examined the glass glistening on the asphalt. "How long were you away from your car?"

"Oh, uh – probably like two hours? Hour and a half? I went on a hike."

That explained her outfit – it seemed a bit light for the weather. She looked...well, nice. Like she always did, but more outdoorsy than usual. Her cheeks were flushed red and her ponytail looked a bit wind-whipped. "Did you see anyone else while you were hiking?"

She shrugged. "No, not really. When I first started out, there were some people hanging out at the lighthouse. And then..."

"Were you here with anyone?"

"No, I was by myself."

"Oh, okay." He leaned down to look under the car, but there was nothing except more glass. One time when he was investigating a burglarized car, he'd found the crumpled up report card of a high school student. People tended to drop things when they were committing crimes – but this time they had no such luck.

"I don't want to sound crazy," she continued. "But at times, I felt like there might have been someone else out on the trail."

Matthew raised himself off of the ground. "You mean following you?"

"I mean...not exactly? But I kept thinking there was someone creeping around, but then when I'd look, I couldn't see anything."

Matthew nodded. "I see."

"But actually, that's really silly, and I was probably imagining it."

"No, it's good to note. You never know," he replied.

He was about to ask another question when he noticed that she was shivering.

"Are you okay?" he asked. "Are you cold?"

She waved a hand. "No, I'm fine. It's just – I was walking so fast on the trail and now that I've been stopped for a while, I'm cooling off."

"Listen – how about you get into my car and get warmed up." He paused, taking his coat off to offer to her, which she accepted. "Actually, I don't live too far from here; I have a shop-vac that we can use for the glass. And then you can either drive your car home or I can have it towed. It's up to you."

"I really don't want to be a bother," Jade said, her teeth chattering.

"It's no problem at all. C'mon, please," he opened the passenger door. "Before you freeze to death."

She hesitated but ultimately relented, taking a seat.

Matthew got in and started the engine. "Is there anything that you need to grab out of your car before we go? Anything valuable?"

She shook her head. "No. I didn't even really check to see if they stole anything yet. There wasn't anything good in there. I'm not even sure what they were looking for."

"We see it a lot, especially in parking lots. People break in looking for all kinds of stuff – cell phones, headphones, even spare change."

"Oh. That kind of kills my theory that there was someone else creeping around."

Matthew smiled. "Well, no. You could be targeted for some reason. Do you have any enemies that you know of?"

Jade laughed. "Where do I start?"

"Well, I know one guy who I'll be questioning."

Jade looked at him with a look of confusion. "Brandon? Oh – I don't think that he would do this."

"Maybe, maybe not." Matthew didn't know the guy well, but the one time that he arrested him for threatening Jade during their divorce mediation was pretty eye-opening. "Who else?"

Jade stretched her hands out to warm them over the vents. Matthew had to remind himself not to stare.

"I think that's the only one, not that I'd call him an enemy exactly," she said. "Oh – I guess Morgan has some enemies. You know, with her mom's case. Maybe Andrea hired someone from jail to get revenge for getting her arrested?"

Matthew laughed. "That's...not impossible."

"Or maybe her boyfriend Brock did something? I don't know that this is his style, though. Or that he would come after *me*."

Matthew nodded. "Might be worth investigating, though. I'll look into it."

"Oh!" she turned towards him. "Well – this seems really silly, actually. But Barb McFarland told me to keep my nose out of where it doesn't belong. Or out of her business, or something."

"What?" Matthew turned towards her. "That sounds – I mean, was that a threat?"

Jade closed her eyes and let out a little laugh. "Well no, I don't think so. I don't think she meant it like that."

"What did you do to her? And who is she?"

"She's the president of the San Juan Small Business Association."

"Oh."

"And – well, it's a long story. But I started getting involved with the San Juan County Council."

Matthew had to keep himself from smiling. He hadn't seen Jade in weeks or talked to her, truly talked to her, in months. Is this what she'd been up to all this time?

"Did you hear about the twenty-six acres of land that Colby Smith left to San Juan Island in his will?"

"Yeah – I heard something about that."

"Well, it turns out that the county council has to decide what to *do* with that land. And almost immediately after it was announced, a developer showed up and offered to buy it for a ton of money. They want to build some kind of luxury resort, I don't know. But I put in a proposal that we should have a vote to decide what happens to it."

"Ah," Matthew said. "I'm guessing you were successful in this?"

"I was," Jade said, a smile tugging at the corner of her mouth. "And now I have two months to convince the people of

San Juan County that the land is better used for the *public* good, and not just something for rich tourists."

"That sounds awesome, actually. But I'm sure that the developers don't agree."

Jade nodded. "Right. And neither does Barb. But everyone has a chance to make their case! I just…didn't think it was right for it to be sold like that. Colby said he wanted to leave it to his neighbors."

Matthew pulled his car into the driveway in front of his house. "You're right. But now you're also up to roughly ten potential enemies."

Jade laughed. "I don't think so. I think I was just being paranoid. I bet it was just some high school kids or something."

He wasn't as convinced, but decided to keep that to himself for now. "Also a possibility. Anyway, welcome to my humble abode. It's not much, and you don't have to come inside if you don't want to, I can just grab the vacuum and – "

"No – I mean, I don't want to barge in on your house or anything. But I feel like I should at least help with the clean up."

Matthew certainly wasn't going to let Jade do any of the heavy lifting, but he also didn't want to force her to sit out in the car by herself. "Okay, then great. You can meet my new dog."

Jade's face lit up. "You got a dog?"

He nodded. "Yeah. It's a long story; we took him out of a bad situation. He was neglected, maybe a bit abused."

"Aw, poor thing. And then you decided to keep him?"

Matthew got out of the car and Jade followed. "Yeah. I took him home that first night because animal control was closed. And after that…I couldn't stand to drop him off. He's had it bad enough and just needs a bit of a hand, you know?"

"I can't wait to meet him!" she said as they approached the front door.

Matthew pulled out his keys. "Uh, actually, I don't get a lot of visitors. So don't be afraid if he barks at you at first; usually he'll bark before he runs away and hides."

"That's alright, I don't mind."

Almost as if on cue, furious barking started as soon as he pushed the door open. Matthew flicked on a light.

"It's okay buddy, calm down."

Jade slowly followed behind. "Oh my gosh, he's *beautiful*!" She lowered her voice. "What's his name?"

"I call him Toast."

Toast was now retreating into the living room, still barking but not quite as much.

"Did you come up with that yourself?"

Matthew knelt, hoping that Toast would come over and calm down. "I did. The first night when I brought him home, I left him in the living room while I went to change out of my uniform. When I came back, I found him in the kitchen licking the toaster. He'd got his paws onto the counter, pulled the plug out of the wall, and had it turned upside down on the floor. He was trying to eat the crumbs that fell out."

Jade laughed. "Sounds like a perfect name, actually."

Matthew smiled to himself. He *did* sort of look like a "Toast." He had golden fur, except for some black at his mouth and around his eyes – it almost looked like he was wearing eye liner. Matthew thought he was gorgeous, but usually people were afraid of his deep and relentless barking.

Not Jade. Toast stopped barking and instead cautiously inched closer to her. Without looking at him, she lowered the back of her hand to his nose level.

He let out a low grumble at first, but then leaned forward to get a sniff.

"Wow – I've had him for a few weeks and so far, no one could get near him except for me."

Jade's face lit up again. "Really? Do you think he likes me?"

Toast finished sniffing her hand and his entire posture changed. He dropped his ears, wagged his tail and greeted Matthew normally – by jumping up and trying to lick him.

"Toast – no jumping. Down! *Down!*"

He relented and sat obediently, his tail wagging and causing his whole body to wiggle.

Matthew bent down to pet him, "And yeah! He really does seem to like you. Normally he won't let anyone get into the house without barking at their every move."

"That's good, because I like him too." Jade lowered herself to the ground and Toast immediately went to her, licking her hands and sniffing around her ears and neck. She burst into laughter, which only encouraged him.

Huh. That was a first. Now truthfully, Matthew didn't have a ton of people over. He was still spending more time working than socializing. But maybe everyone else he'd invited over was a jerk. Or maybe Toast just knew when he met someone worth knowing.

"Okay, let me grab my vacuum. Do you want anything to eat or drink?"

She shook her head. "No, I'm okay. But thank you."

"Alright, I'll be back in a minute."

Matthew went into the basement, his head still spinning from Toast's complete acceptance of Jade. What was it about her? Maybe it was that she let Toast come to her – that seemed to work well. And maybe he could tell that Jade wouldn't hurt him – or anyone, for that matter.

But it did seem like someone might be trying to hurt *her*. It could've been a random break-in, sure. But the parks weren't busy at this time of year, and who was hanging around Lime Kiln at night just hoping that there might be a few stray hikers?

Brandon could definitely be involved. Or Andrea. Or anyone, really, who didn't like Jade getting in the way of their business dealings.

Whoever it was, Matthew was going to figure it out and make sure that nothing like that happened to Jade again.

Chapter 3

That evening, after Matthew vacuumed all of the broken glass, Jade was able to drive her car home. She had felt like a doofus just standing there while he worked, but he refused to let her do anything. He was exceedingly polite. He also had insisted on following her home, reasoning that he wanted to make sure that she got back safely and that nothing else was done to her car.

Jade was embarrassed by it all, but she chalked it up to Matthew being a consummate professional. Everything that he did was steady, unhurried and completed with a smile.

Really, it was Jade's fault for saying that she thought someone had followed her during her hike. There was no basis for that – it was just her being paranoid. It could've been the wind or a squirrel or something.

But then Matthew had to take her seriously, despite the fact that she was probably overreacting. Brandon always said that she overreacted; she was trying to change that, but sometimes, her worrying still got the better of her.

Within two days, Jade was able to get her car window fixed and everything seemed to be back to normal. Better than normal, actually, because on Wednesday night, she had the first official meeting for her unofficial committee to make their case for the Colby land vote.

So far, the only people who agreed to be on the committee were her mom, Morgan, and Luke (who was forced to join by

Morgan). It wasn't many people, but they still had some power.

Her mom got the idea to host a fundraiser at the barn at Saltwater Cove. Morgan kept saying that she had lots of connections that would be useful – but hadn't had a chance to elaborate yet. And Luke volunteered to make a video to promote their cause.

Jade worked from home during the day on Wednesday while Morgan and Luke went to the mainland to buy some photography supplies. About an hour before they were due to be back, Jade started making a large batch of chocolate chip cookies.

She'd already made a white chocolate raspberry cheesecake the night before; all she had to do was pull it out of the fridge when they got back. The cookies were an additional touch – there was a certain mood that she wanted to set for the committee, and chewy, warm cookies would be a huge help.

Just after she got the cookies into the oven, she thought that she heard a noise – like a door slamming, or maybe a window? She froze, fear snapping back as though it had never left her since Lime Kiln.

Her heart raced. What was she supposed to do? She took a deep breath and forced herself to think. It sounded like it came from down the hall or one of the bedrooms. Maybe something had fallen over in her room? Or maybe it was something outside, blown over by the wind?

She told herself to stop having an overactive imagination and go investigate; but as she took a step out of the kitchen, she felt her phone vibrating in her pocket. Her heart jumped – it was Matthew.

"Hello?" she whispered.

"Hey! How're you doing? I just wanted to check in."

Jade bit her lip. That was some uncanny timing. "Oh – that's nice of you – I'm okay, everything's fine. I was able to have my window fixed."

"That was fast. Are you sure everything's okay? You sound a little...stressed?"

Well shoot. Why didn't she disguise her voice better? She couldn't lie to him. "Well weirdly...I think my imagination is running wild because I thought I heard something in the house just now."

"What? Really? You know what, I'm nearby – how about I stop over and check it out?"

"No, it's really fine – it's not a big deal. I think I'm just spooked from last weekend."

"I insist, I'm already driving in your direction. Better safe than sorry, right?"

Jade took a frantic look around the kitchen – it was a mess! Not to mention, *she* was a mess! "Yeah, sure! I appreciate it. I'll see you in a second – I just need to, uh, finish up some baking."

"Oh – okay. I'll be there soon."

"Okay!"

No!

Jade wasn't ready to see Matthew! Her hair was crazy, she was wearing sweatpants, and the kitchen was a disaster. She frantically threw some things into the dishwasher and the sink before wiping down the counters.

She ripped off her sweatpants and was about to run into her bedroom to change when she froze – what if someone really *was* in there? And she went barging in without any pants on?

She paused at the door and listened. She couldn't hear anything – it was totally silent.

"You're just being paranoid," she muttered to herself before pushing the door open.

Still, she held her breath for a moment when the door opened, but there was nothing out of the ordinary. The light was on, which was odd, but maybe she'd forgotten to turn it off?

There was no time to think about that now. She dug out a pair of jeans and threw on a different top – something that didn't have flour and water splashed onto it. She then stood in front of the mirror and managed to brush her hair and make a neater ponytail before she heard a knock on the door.

Man, he was fast.

"I'm coming!" she yelled before taking one last look at herself in the mirror. It's not that she was terribly vain, but Matthew had seen her far too many times in a disheveled state. He really was going to start thinking she was crazy if she couldn't *occasionally* look put together.

She pulled the door open to find him standing in his sheriff's uniform. It didn't matter how many times she saw him in the uniform...every time she felt a little stunned.

"Hey, thanks for stopping by. Come on in."

"Any time." He stepped inside, towering over her. He looked even taller in her own house for some reason. "So what happened?"

"Well," she said, trying to keep her tone even, "I was baking and I heard something – again, it was probably nothing. But now that it got into my head that someone might be unhappy with me, I just think that I'm a little – you know, paranoid."

"You're not paranoid. I think you have every reason to be cautious. Where do you think the noise came from?"

"Oh – I think back in my bedroom, but I already went and looked and no one was there."

"Can I take a look?" he asked.

"Sure."

She led him back to her room and as soon as she opened the door, realized with horror that her sweatpants were sprawled across the floor. She tried to casually pick them up. "Sorry for the mess."

He smiled politely. "It's not messy at all. Much cleaner than my house the other night. And as much as I like to blame any mess on the dog, he really only goes after the toaster."

Jade laughed and watched as he slowly walked around the room before getting to the back window.

"Where does this go?"

"To the backyard."

"You don't have a second floor, right?"

"Right."

He used one hand and lifted the window open. "Do you always leave this unlocked?"

Jade frowned. "I don't think so? I didn't know it was open..."

"Hmm. Okay. And did you know that your garage door is open?"

Jade stopped. "It is?"

Matthew nodded. "Yeah – wide open, and your car's on the street."

"Yeah, that's because the guy that we rent this house from was supposed to clear out the garage. He has a bunch of stuff in there that he's storing – but he hasn't gotten around to it and we can't even fit a car in there."

Matthew narrowed his eyes. "Interesting. So you didn't open the garage door today?"

Jade shook her head. "No, not on purpose. Unless Morgan did? But she's been gone all day."

"Do you have a garage door opener in your car?"

"I do..."

Matthew nodded. "It's not uncommon for openers to be stolen when cars are broken into. And then the burglars use it to gain access to the home."

Jade gasped. "I never even thought of that! Hold on – let me go outside and check my car."

Jade put on shoes and Matthew followed her outside. She gasped again. "Oh my gosh! It's gone. I had it on the visor, I didn't even notice it was missing!"

"So I don't want to scare you," Matthew said with a sigh. "But it does seem like someone may have gotten into your house today. They might've assumed that you weren't home and when they heard you..."

Jade's hand darted to her mouth. "They jumped out of the window and into the backyard?"

Matthew nodded. "That would explain why they didn't close the garage. You didn't hear it open?"

"No. It's pretty quiet. And I was working until recently; I wear headphones so I can drown out any distractions."

At that moment, Morgan pulled into the driveway. Jade tried not to allow her face to look too concerned about the terrifying discovery they just made, but she didn't know how well she was succeeding.

"Hey, it's a party in the driveway!" Morgan yelled.

"Should I put on some music?" asked Luke.

Jade forced herself to smile. "Hey guys. How was your shopping trip?"

"It was fine. What's up Matthew? Did Jade's car get broken into again?"

Matthew's eyes darted between Morgan and Jade before he responded. "Well no – not exactly. But I think that someone may have gotten into the house just now."

Morgan gasped. "Are you serious! Are you joking with me right now?"

Jade shook her head. "I'm afraid not. My head's spinning."

"Why don't we discuss this inside," suggested Luke. "I believe I was promised a cheesecake and I don't see it out here."

Morgan shot him an annoyed look but agreed. "Yeah, it's kinda cold. Let's go inside. If it's even safe in there!"

Matthew laughed. "I think it's okay."

"Well, Matthew *does* have a gun," said Luke as he walked towards the door. "And he agreed to allow me to use it. You know, if something happens to him. I can protect us."

"Right," Morgan said flatly.

They went inside and Jade caught them up on the events of the evening as she pulled the cookies out of the oven. She was worried that they might have been a bit overbaked in all the excitement, but she removed them from the baking sheet and they seemed to retain their chewy quality.

For about an hour, they went back and forth about the burglary and checked every room in the house. Nothing seemed to be missing. Matthew said that the person probably didn't expect Jade to be home.

"How'd they know where I lived, though?"

Morgan crossed her arms. "Don't you have your insurance and registration in the glove box?"

Jade frowned. "Doesn't everyone?"

"I guess." Morgan said. "So this guy kind of got in the house, and then ran away without stealing anything? I, for one, think this criminal is as dumb as a bag of rocks, and I'm sick of talking about him. I'm here for a committee meeting about Colby Farm."

Jade smiled but said nothing. Morgan was probably right. She was silly to feel so unnerved by it all; nothing *actually* bad happened.

"And I'm here for a cheesecake," added Luke. "Matthew, are you just going to stay here and enjoy Jade's baking without contributing?"

Matthew shook his head. "I'm happy to contribute. I'm off the clock."

"Excellent!" said Morgan. "Then you can help us."

Jade shot her a look. "I'm sure that he doesn't want to be involved in our committee."

"Is it the cheesecake and cookie committee?" asked Matthew.

"It isn't," said Luke, "but if I'm honest, that's probably going to be a *huge* factor for my participation."

"I'd be delighted to be part of the committee with or without cake," said Matthew.

"Great!" Morgan replied. "Because we have a lot of ideas and we need a lot of help."

"Do we?" said Jade, eyeing her.

"Yes! Hold on a second." Morgan walked out of the room and returned with a large poster board. "I put this together last night."

"Wow, that looks really nice." Jade stood up to get a better look – there were several categories and it was even color coded.

"Surprisingly pretty, I know," commented Luke. "I'll have to take credit for the scheme here, we – "

"Quiet you." Morgan set the poster board in his hands and motioned for him to stand up. "Okay, so here I have our main goals. We have two months to come up with ideas for the property, raise awareness about the vote, and also raise some funds to show that we'd be able to develop the land into something if we had the chance."

"Right," Jade said slowly. "So, basically, we just have to do everything."

Morgan nodded "Right! And don't worry, little by little, we can get everything done. I have a friend who I told about this and she volunteered to make some digital mockups on the land."

Jade frowned. "That's really nice of her, but how are we going to pay her? I wouldn't want her to do it for free."

"Believe me," Morgan waved a hand, "I offered to pay her and she wouldn't accept it. She's a real sucker. Kinda like you."

Jade narrowed her eyes. "What's that supposed to mean?"

Morgan flashed a smile and continued. "She said that she already has a bunch of stuff built so it's really easy for her to just throw it into a new landscape and make it look realistic. Don't worry, it'll be really good, and she does the renderings digitally so Luke can use part of it in his video. I was thinking he could also do a bit of a merge, like with some aerial footage and upbeat music..."

"Yes, yes, don't worry – I'll handle the video. You don't want Morgan getting involved. Her idea of upbeat music is the synthesized version of a recorder."

Jade groaned. "I know."

"And Margie said that we can host a fundraiser at the barn!" Morgan said as she clapped her hands together. "That'll be great – I'm thinking like a masquerade ball? I've always wanted to go to a masquerade ball."

"Uh..." Jade tried to find a gentle way to weigh in. "I don't know that people will be as excited as you are to go to a masquerade ball."

"We *could* put 'mask optional' on the invitation," said Luke. "You know – black tie optional, mask optional."

"Sure," Jade said. "We'll figure it out."

She could already tell that this project was getting out of her control. It wasn't that she was against sharing control, exactly. She was just...scared about taking it on in general. Maybe she wasn't the right person for the job?

They spent the next hour brainstorming ideas and ended up assigning everyone a task. Jade felt odd making Matthew do anything – it seemed like he was too polite to say no – so she gave him something easy. His task was to talk to the rest of the sheriff department staff and get them excited about the idea. It was lame, sure – but Jade didn't want to inconvenience him.

After the boys left, Morgan and Jade spent some time tidying up. Within five minutes, Morgan started her teasing.

"So...Matthew just decided to drop by?"

"Actually, it was kind of weird – right after I heard the window close, he called me. It was odd timing."

"Oh," cooed Morgan. "Do you think it's really just been Matthew all along? Breaking into your car, then into our house so he could play rescuer?"

Jade couldn't help but laugh – the thought was so ridiculous. "No, unfortunately I think it actually *was* someone else doing all of those things. It doesn't seem like they managed to steal anything, though. And Matthew disconnected the garage door opener, so they shouldn't be able to get in again before we can get a new opener."

Morgan raised an eyebrow. "I hope not. But just in case, you'd better keep Matthew close. You know, for protection."

"Sure," Jade said casually. "He's a good friend to have."

"Oh, uh huh. *Right.*"

Jade stopped what she was doing and stared at her. "*Right* what?"

"Nothing!"

"You can say it. Just go ahead and say whatever it is that you want to say."

"What?" Morgan insisted. "I don't want to say anything!"

Jade let out a sigh. "Come on, just do it. You've been giving me weird vibes all night."

"Oh, you picked up on that?" Morgan smiled. "I *was* laying it on pretty thick. Alright, I just kind of, sort of, think you two get along really well."

"And?"

"And if you like him, it wouldn't be the *worst* thing in the world. He seems like a nice guy."

Jade rolled her eyes. "Lots of guys *seem* like they're nice guys."

"Oh come *on*," said Morgan. "You can't pretend that Matthew is some hidden creep. I was only joking about him breaking into your car because it's so absurd."

Jade paused. "I know. But..."

"But what?"

She took a deep breath. "That's all he is. He's just nice. I don't think he has any...romantic feelings towards me."

"I disagree," Morgan said simply. "I think him checking up on you and staying to be part of the committee means something."

"Really?"

"Of course!" Morgan said, turning to face her. "And you're smart, and pretty, and fun. Why wouldn't he like you?"

Jade wanted to hide her embarrassment and turned to wash some dishes. "Well, that's nice of you to say. Either way, he's good to have around. Especially when someone is messing with us like this."

"Don't worry," Morgan said, picking up a towel to dry the dishes. "I think our troubles are over with that. They won't be able to break in again so easily. But if you want to call Matthew and tell him you're scared…"

"*Morgan,*" Jade groaned. "I'm not going to do that!"

"Okay, okay! I was just, you know, brainstorming!"

"Thanks for that," Jade said, handing her a baking sheet. "But let's keep the brainstorming on the project for now?"

"Fine," Morgan said with a smile.

Jade turned back to the dishes. She didn't want to get a big head, but what if Morgan was right? What if Matthew really *did* like her?

Maybe he was a nice guy. He certainly pulled off a uniform like no one else. And at the very least, he had a great dog. That had to count for something.

Chapter 4

On Friday night, Matthew volunteered to help Chief set up alarms at Morgan and Jade's place. It was all being done at Margie's insistence, and the most that Jade would agree to were a few contact alarms. Matthew was happy to help – and happy for an excuse to see Jade again.

"Mom," Jade said gently. "I really don't think you have to worry so much."

"I've always worried! All I do is worry! Are you *sure* that you don't want to set up some cameras? Just a few?"

Matthew suppressed a smile, trying to channel his focus onto the sensor that he was attaching for the living room window. He was trying to pretend like he wasn't listening, but it was hard.

"I really don't think that's necessary right now," said Jade. "But if something else happens, we can revisit it."

"If something else happens, you could get hurt!" Margie replied.

"Don't worry, I won't." Jade walked close to Matthew and dropped her voice. "If you thought that *I* was paranoid, you can at least see where I get it from."

Matthew smiled. He didn't think that Jade was paranoid at all. She was being surprisingly coolheaded after having someone break into her home. "You get a lot of good qualities from your mom."

Jade let out a small laugh. "You're right. Like baking!"

"That's one," he said as he drilled in the last screw in the window frame.

"I made some lemon bars, by the way – they're in the kitchen. Do you want to take a break? Maybe I can finish whatever you're doing up there?"

"This window's done, actually. I think it was the last one."

Jade leaned to get a better look. "So if I accidentally leave one of the sensors on and open the window, the alarm will go off?"

"That's right," said Matthew. "And you'll probably lose hearing for a few weeks."

"Wonderful," Jade said with a smile. "Well – I'm really doing this for my mom. She's been freaked out about everything."

"Yes I have!" yelled Margie from the other room. "And you should be worried too!"

Jade put her hands up. "I *am* worried! Look how worried I am! I'm going to live with deafening alarms."

"Good," said Margie.

Matthew and Jade shared a look, both trying not to laugh.

Chief popped his head into the room. "I just have one more alarm for the kitchen window – that is, if you want it?"

"No, that's – "

Margie cut Jade off. "Of *course* she wants it! But honey, we really need to get going."

"Oh, it'll only take a minute."

"No – maybe Matthew can do it for us? Would you mind, Matthew?"

Matthew shook his head. "Oh, no – I don't mind at all."

"Where're you going mom?" asked Jade.

"Yeah honey, where are we going?" Chief replied. "Is it that quilting class that you signed up for?"

Jade crossed her arms. "I didn't know that you signed up for a quilting class. Where is it?"

"Never mind that, we have to go! Honey, I love you, stay safe! I'll see you Sunday for dinner, right?"

"Of course."

"And you too, Matthew! Not working this Sunday I hope?"

Matthew shook his head. "No, I'm not working. I'd love to come."

Margie beamed. "Great! We'll see you then. Call me if anything happens – anything at all!"

Chief barely managed to hand off the sensor before Margie dragged him out the door.

"She's been acting strange lately," commented Jade. "I don't know what's going on with her."

"Oh?" said Matthew. If he didn't know any better, he'd say that Margie was trying to orchestrate a reason for him and Jade to be alone together. In fact, some might say it was the most obvious thing in the world, and that it wasn't the first time she'd done it. "I didn't notice. Let me get the sensor up for you."

"Oh, thank you. I really can do it myself, I don't know why my mom insisted on making you guys do it."

"Probably," Matthew said as he found a spot for the sensor. "Because she knew that you *could* do it yourself, but you *wouldn't* do it yourself."

Jade laughed. "Fair point."

Matthew carefully aligned the first screw and attached it to the window. "I'm not sure how happy your landlord is going to be about all these holes that we've made."

"I asked him. He doesn't mind. He offered to come do it himself actually."

"Huh. What a nice guy." He drilled in the second hole. Jade *would* have a nice landlord. Nice people like Jade always ended up surrounded by other nice people. Matthew's landlord wouldn't even fix his fridge and his food was constantly close to going bad.

"Yeah, he is really nice. He just has a hard time with clutter, hence the garage."

"I see."

Matthew put his hands on his hips. That was the last thing he could install. Should he announce that he was done and that he needed to leave? Or did Margie know something that he didn't?

Maybe that Jade...wanted to spend some time with him?

That would be too good to be true. He could try...asking her to dinner? He'd asked her to see that comedian a few months ago, and she'd flat out turned him down.

He'd taken that as a hint that she wasn't interested, but it seemed like Margie was always coming up with excuses for them to be together.

That could be Margie just being Margie. But what if it was more than that?

At the exact moment when Matthew took a step forward, Jade spun around with a lemon bar in her hand. Almost in slow motion, they collided in the middle of the kitchen, the lemon bar bouncing off of Matthew's chest and landing with a splat on the floor.

"I'm *so* sorry!" said Jade, her hand darting to her mouth.

Matthew dusted his shirt off. "It's okay, I'm sorry that I slammed into you like that. Are you okay?"

They made their next move in unison as well – crouching down to grab the lemon bar.

"Oh, sorry, I can clean it," Jade said.

They both reached forward, briefly brushing hands. It seemed like Jade lingered for a moment. Or was he imagining it?

"Ah, sorry," Matthew said with an awkward laugh. "You can't make such sudden movements around me, I think we're seconds away from hitting heads and getting mutual concussions."

"I think you're right."

Their eyes met, and they both laughed before looking away. Matthew rarely got to look into her beautiful eyes for long...

She looked back at him again. Something came over him – the moment was too perfect to ignore. What if he just slowly leaned forward, and their lips happened to meet and...

As soon as he was a few inches closer to her, Jade turned her head, scooped up the lemon bar, and stood up. It was over before he even knew what happened.

He stayed on the floor for a moment, feeling a shock run through his body. Not just for what he had almost done, but also because of the way she reacted.

Wow.

That was bad.

That was really *really* bad.

He stood up. "I'm sorry about that, I didn't mean to – "

"No it's okay, I have plenty." Jade outstretched her hand; on it was a napkin with a non-smashed lemon bar. "Would you like one?"

"Thanks, but I'm good. I have to get going actually."

"Oh, alright. Thank you so much for your help."

"Of course, anytime. Take care."

"You too."

Matthew made his way out the door and drove home, berating himself the entire way. *What* was he thinking? Why would he think that Jade wanted to kiss him? And why would he do it like *that*?

Never in his life had he tried to kiss someone out of the blue like that. Never! What possessed him to think that now was the time to start?

Yes, he'd been seeing a lot of her lately. And she was pretty and exceedingly kind and...

Ugh.

He should've stuck with his original plan of asking her to dinner. No, he should've just...left her alone. She'd never done anything to suggest that she liked him; she'd just been forced to interact with him recently because someone broke into her car and then into her home.

Then he came along and instead of trying to help her, he crossed a line.

He went home that night and tried to distract himself from his shame and embarrassment by taking Toast for a long walk. It was hard not to think about it, though. How could he have been so stupid?

His only friends on the island were all connected to Jade. If he randomly kissed her without warning and ruined their friendship, he'd lose *all* of those friendships. Morgan, Luke... even Margie and Chief would feel strange around him.

Matthew went to work the next morning with a plan to focus and keep his mind busy. Around noon he got a call about a suspected drunk driver who was weaving all over the road. Matthew found the car quickly, and it turned out to be a lady with diabetes whose blood sugar had dropped severely low. They were able to get her to the hospital and get her taken care of. She was extremely grateful, and that made Matthew feel a bit better. At least he wasn't a *complete* failure.

On the way home from work, his mom called. She usually didn't call him unless something was wrong, so he picked up immediately. "Hello?"

"Hi, it's me. How are you?"

"I'm good Mom. What's up? Is something wrong? How's Dad?"

"Everything is okay, don't worry. Sorry, I guess I should've started with that."

"No, it's okay. Glad to hear it."

Matthew felt his grip loosen on the phone. His dad had a massive stroke a few months back. It was a total shock – he'd always been relatively healthy, tried to watch what he ate, and even exercised a bit. The stroke left him completely unable to use his left arm.

Matthew went home for three weeks to help out; his dad was lucky enough to get into an intensive rehab, and his progress was unbelievable. He was back to mostly being able to take care of himself. But now Matthew was always worried that something would happen again – and he'd be thousands of miles away, unable to help.

"So...what's up?" he asked.

"Oh, you know, same old. You know that new neighbor I told you about?"

"Yeah."

"Well I had to send her a letter. She's been doing her trash wrong and it's driving me insane."

Matthew sighed. "That was nice of you."

"Well how else will she know? I also mentioned that they need to plant some grass, their front yard is *very* muddy."

"You could plant it for her if it bothers you so much."

"What?"

He debated repeating himself, but decided against it. There was no need to start an argument. "Nothing."

"So...have you heard from Laura recently?"

There it was. "No Mom, I can't say that I have."

"Oh."

"Why?"

"Well, you know how much I've always liked her. And after your dad was sick, she was so helpful – she brought over so many wonderful dishes and offered to stay with him if I had to run to the store..."

"Mom," Matthew said. "There's a reason that she's my *ex*-girlfriend. I'm glad that she was nice, but – "

"But what? You need to remember that a girl like that doesn't come along very often."

"I'll keep that in mind."

"Unless...you have a new girlfriend you're not telling me about?"

Oof. If only she knew. "No, that's not the case."

"Oh! Well I have to run! Take care, come visit soon!"

"Bye Mom."

That was weird. She liked to bring up Laura every couple of weeks, but she'd never specifically called *just* to talk about her. Something must've set her off.

Matthew got back to his house and was surprised to see a car in the driveway. He parked on the street and walked over, shining his light into the driver's side.

The driver turned around, trying to shield her eyes. His stomach dropped.

It was Laura.

Of course.

Chapter 5

Did that really happen? Did Matthew really just try to *kiss* her?

Jade couldn't decide. She spent the rest of the evening replaying everything in her head. For a while, she had herself convinced that it wasn't what it looked like; he seemed to be leaning forward, but he could've just been trying to stand up or something.

But why did she have to freak out and jump away like that?

Maybe it didn't look *that* dorky to him. They'd already come close to bumping heads, so maybe he thought she was just avoiding that. Really, though...a small part of her brain thought he was trying to kiss her, and she panicked.

But no, that didn't make any sense when she really thought about it. Why would Matthew want to kiss *her*?

They got into a weird position, that was all. And he was trying to get up, and so was she, and it was just awkward. Nothing more.

Despite that, for the entire weekend, she couldn't bring herself to tell Morgan about it. She didn't trust herself to even describe it accurately. The more she thought about it, though, the more it bothered her that she cared so much.

Jade kept running through the same thoughts all weekend. She finally decided that it didn't matter if Matthew was going to kiss her or not – what mattered was if she actually *wanted* him to kiss her.

Her own feelings on it really gave her a clue into her psyche. Greta would be so proud when she heard how honest Jade was trying to be with herself.

Jade knew that as much as she said again and again that she needed to stay single so that she could piece her life back together, the truth was...well, the truth was undeniable now. Deep down, in a silly school girl way, she actually *wanted* it to be true that Matthew was trying to kiss her.

But she also knew that it was *probably* just wishful thinking. Even admitting it to herself made her feel giddy. She wasn't ready to say it out loud, so she decided to keep that giddy feeling to herself. But it was nice – she hadn't felt good or excited about a guy in ages.

It didn't hurt that Matthew volunteered to join her committee as well. So at the very least, she'd get to spend some time with him. Kiss or no kiss, it made her feel young again, or something.

Excitingly, Matthew was coming to Sunday dinner that week too. Jade decided to get a little extra done up – nothing wild, but she made sure that her hair wasn't in a frazzled ponytail. She actually had time to straighten it for once. She spent a little extra time putting on her makeup, and she decided to wear a green top that made her eyes pop. Or at least that was what Morgan always said about it.

To her relief, Morgan didn't make any comments about her appearance on the way to dinner. Instead, she talked a mile a minute about Luke's progress on the video and her friend's renderings of what could be built on Colby's land.

"Are you going to let me see it, or are you going to keep it a secret?" asked Jade.

"I'm waiting to debut it until we're at dinner," Morgan replied.

"Such a flair for the dramatic."

"Listen," Morgan said with a smile, "I'm trying to funnel my dramatic energy into something positive."

"Oh, in that case," Jade said, "the county thanks you."

Jade was happy to have Morgan's help – Morgan was really good at stuff like this. With minimal advertising, she already had a huge growth in her photography business. Yet despite being busy, she was more than happy to put a *lot* of time into Jade's new project. Her can-do attitude was always useful when there was a daunting task; and the entire project only seemed more and more daunting by the day.

They got to her mom's house and said their hellos. Jade volunteered to make dessert that week and decided to stick with a classic apple pie. She felt a little nervous, actually, to see Matthew again. Her big idea was to invite him for drinks and to thank him for joining her committee. Surely he could say no if he wasn't interested?

But hopefully...he wouldn't say no.

Luke arrived not long after they got there, and Morgan started questioning him right away.

"I thought you were bringing Matthew?" Morgan asked.

Jade worried that Matthew might've backed out. Maybe he was mad at her. Maybe he really *was* trying to kiss her and she'd hurt his feelings?

How could she bring it up to him without embarrassing them both? It was risky, especially if this was all in her head. Between this and the imagining people following her, he was going to think she was totally nuts.

"Oh, he said that he could drive himself. He also said that he was bringing someone?" Luke looked around the room.

Morgan narrowed her eyes. "Bringing who?"

"I was hoping you knew," he said.

"That was my doing," Chief Hank chimed in. "I ran into him in Friday Harbor earlier today and he was with a girl. I asked him if he was coming tonight and extended the invitation to her, too."

Morgan crossed her arms. "Was this his sister or something, Chief?"

He shrugged. "I don't know, I didn't ask. She seemed very excited by it."

A girl. Of course.

Matthew wasn't interested in her – he had someone else. He was just trying to be nice to her because she was a crazy old spinster imagining that people were out to get her.

Her mom marched into the dining room with her hands on her hips. "What's this? Matthew's bringing a girl? Is this his girlfriend?"

Luke put his hands up. "I don't know anything about a girlfriend. I'm not involved, this is all Chief's fault."

Her mom continued. "Hank, why would you go and do a thing like this?"

Chief Hank looked around, clearly surprised by the reaction he was getting. "I don't know, I was being friendly? I'm not sure why you're mad at *me!* You were supposed to meet me in town, this is your fault."

"*My fault!* You're blaming me because I wasn't there to stop you?"

"I wasn't *blaming* you," Chief Hank said as he slowly backed away. "But if you don't want me doing things that you don't want me to do, you have to supervise me a little more closely. Where were you anyway?"

"I – had to run some errands! This isn't about me! I didn't think you'd be out there inviting people left and right!"

There was a knock on the door and the room fell silent.

Jade had the urge to flee but stood, frozen.

After a moment, Morgan motioned to Luke. "He's *your* friend! Go let him in!"

"I have no idea why I'm being yelled at for this," he said as he walked toward the door. "This is clearly the fault of the police chief."

Morgan shushed him and motioned for him to open the door.

He winked at her before finally doing as he was told. "Hello! Matthew, so nice to see you, and who is this lovely lady?"

"Hey Luke, this is Laura. Luke is my – "

"Hi Luke, it's nice to finally meet you. I'm Laura, Matthew's girlfriend."

They stepped inside and Jade forced herself to keep her facial expression neutral, even though it felt like she'd just been punched in the gut.

Laura was beautiful – she had flowing blonde hair, delicately curled and cascading down her shoulders. She took off her dark blue peacoat to reveal a fitted pink and white flowery dress. Suddenly Jade's green top felt less like an effort to look pretty and more like sad pajamas. She crossed her arms.

Matthew went around the room and introduced Laura to everyone there.

"Oh my gosh, it is *so* nice to meet you all. I have to apologize, I wasn't able to make one of my normal desserts on short notice, but I was able to throw together a little something."

She handed a large glass container to Chief Hank. "This is some of my homemade vanilla ice cream."

"Oh, thanks," he replied. "I'll put this in the freezer. Jade baked an apple pie, so that will go together nicely."

"Oh wow, we're really on the same wavelength!" said Laura, beaming at her.

Jade forced herself to smile. "We are!"

They took their seats at the table, Jade feeling like she was in a bit of a haze. How could she have been so silly and *so* far off about how Matthew felt about her? Not only did he not like her, he definitely wasn't trying to kiss her – he had a girlfriend! How clueless could she be?

Jade had to force herself to zone back into the conversation. Apparently, Laura and Matthew dated for years before he moved to San Juan Island. And now, apparently, they were just reconnecting.

Great.

Laura wasn't being obnoxious or anything. She was just giving their history – talking about how she moved to Anacortes and how excited she was to be living on the West Coast.

"I've never been out here, but I'm just *so* in love with it. And I'm so excited! I feel like a new person."

"That's nice," said Morgan. "Speaking of new people, have I told you guys about Andrea's new lawyer?"

Thank goodness – Morgan was always good for a change in topic. "No, what's going on?"

Morgan cleared her throat. "Well! For those of you who don't know, Andrea is on trial for running my mother over with her car."

Laura gasped but Morgan didn't allow for any questions. Jade bit her lip so she wouldn't smile – normally she didn't like when Morgan was rude or purposely left people out of conversations, but today it was sort of amusing.

"Her first attorney, who I'm sure cost a fortune, wasn't performing to her expectations. So her *new* attorney, who I'm sure costs *two* fortunes, is being pretty aggressive. We're still in the discovery stage of everything."

"It feels like this is taking forever," Jade commented.

"You're telling me!" said Morgan. "It's been months and it feels like we're never going to get to the actual trial. But anyway, the new attorney is challenging the recording that we have of when Andrea confessed her crime to Luke."

"Oh no!" Jade's mom exclaimed. "Does that mean that they won't be able to use it in the trial?"

"That's exactly what it would mean," Morgan said.

Matthew sighed. "We knew that was a risk when we made the recording. I think we were all just hoping that she would plead guilty."

"No such luck," said Morgan. "So if that gets thrown out, the only evidence that we really have is Luke's testimony when she confessed."

"And of course," said Luke holding out a hand. "I will refuse to provide any evidence and plead the fifth."

Morgan shot him a look. "You have to stop making that joke, it isn't even funny."

"Sorry, I thought it was kind of fun? You know, adding some drama and flair to the trial?"

Jade smiled. It *was* kind of funny, and she always liked watching Luke push Morgan's buttons.

"You can be funny on your own time, but when you get to the courtroom, your time is mine," said Morgan matter-of-factly. "So yes, all we have is what Luke says when he testifies."

"I don't see the judge letting the recording slide," said Chief Hank. "Don't worry though – keep some faith. The prosecution is doing all that they can for your mom's case."

"Thanks Chief," said Morgan. It seemed like Laura was about to ask a question, but Morgan started talking again. "And in other news, my friend Ahra sent me some preliminary mockups for the Colby Farm project!"

Matthew leaned over to Laura and dropped his voice. "This is that plot of land I was telling you about that we're trying to prevent from being sold off to developers."

Laura's eyes brightened. "Oh, right!"

"I can show them to everyone now? If you'd like to see?"

"We would love to see," Jade said. "You've made me wait all night."

Matthew shot her a smile from across the table that Jade pretended not to see. She was too embarrassed to look him in the eye. Not that he knew how she felt about him, but even so, she didn't want to give it away by staring at him pathetically.

They looked at the renderings and they were quite good. After that, Jade was quiet for the rest of the night until it was time to go home. She tried to act as normal as possible, but she always felt shy around new people.

On the way home, Morgan asked her if she'd known about Laura.

"I didn't, but I'm happy for him. Like you said before, Matthew's a nice guy."

Morgan sighed. "I'm sorry Jade, I really thought that he liked you."

"He does, I think, but as a friend. And that's just fine."

Thankfully, Morgan didn't push the topic anymore. When they got home, Jade got ready for bed and when she was finally alone, she allowed herself to cry a few tears.

She'd been a bit of a fool to get so excited about Matthew – the break-in messed with her head. She made a quiet promise that she wouldn't allow herself to get carried away again.

There was far too much raging in her imagination recently. She had to get her head on straight and focus on something bigger than herself. The vote was only seven weeks away – that was where she needed to spend her time.

Chapter 6

After dinner on Sunday, Matthew dropped Laura off at the ferry terminal.

"I wish we had more time together," she said. "Didn't you say that you were coming to Anacortes sometime this week? Maybe I can make dinner for you."

"Oh – I'm not sure when I'll be there yet. I need to talk to Chief about a few things."

"Well, let me know. I'm free pretty much every night." She let out a little laugh. "You're the only person I know here, other than my coworkers."

Matthew nodded. "I will."

"I'll see you soon?"

"Sure."

She leaned in and gave him a long hug, then a kiss on the cheek, before walking off. He watched her get onto the ferry before getting back into his car. The entire way home, Matthew reflected on how guilty he felt that he was her only friend in the area.

On the one hand, he didn't ask her to move out here. But on the other hand, it seemed like she'd missed him so much that she didn't have a choice.

It wasn't like he had a ton of friends on the island, either. Seeing her was lovely; it was like an echo of home. Even her voice made him feel at ease. He didn't fully realize how homesick he was until he saw her. Yet he was still stunned by the whole situation and didn't quite know how to sort through his thoughts.

When he had found her in his driveway the night prior, he was somewhat alarmed to see her. "Laura – what's going on?"

"So I just moved to Anacortes and was on the island so I figured I'd stop by – actually, maybe we can talk about this inside?"

Oh boy. "Alright."

She followed him to the door; Toast was already barking at the unfamiliar voice.

"Oh no, you got a dog?" asked Laura. "Is he big?"

Matthew shrugged. "About eighty pounds. Don't worry – his bark is worse than his bite."

"He bites?"

Matthew laughed. "No, don't worry, he doesn't. Come on in."

He let her into the living room and offered her a seat on the couch. Toast kept barking, first close-up, and then from far away, popping his head from behind the couch every so often.

"He'll come around eventually," said Matthew.

"You're a *very* pretty boy, aren't you?" Laura said in a high-pitched voice.

Toast growled, then ran off to hide in the kitchen.

"Sorry, he's not really used to attention. I've only had him for a bit."

"That's okay." She cleared her throat. "So, I don't want to take up too much of your time. I don't know if you have plans tonight, or if your girlfriend is coming over…"

Matthew sighed. That was everyone's favorite question. "I don't have a girlfriend."

"Oh!" Laura's face brightened. "Well, I just really needed to talk to you. I've been thinking a lot about what you said – about how you wanted a different life than the one that we were building. So I quit my job, and I got a job up here in Burlington. And I moved to Anacortes."

"Wow." Matthew stared at her for a moment. It was true that he'd said those things when they'd broken up, but he didn't intend for *her* to change. He wanted a different life for himself. "Okay."

"Matty – I want to start over, too. I thought I would take the ferry over and just check out what it looks like over here – and you were *so* right, it's *so* beautiful. I see why you love it up here."

"Yeah, it's really something."

She folded her hands in her lap. "I know this is a lot to drop onto you all at once, but I'm still in love with you. And I know that we had our problems, but I want to see if we could start over together."

Matthew didn't know what to say. She'd sort of kept in touch the past few months, but just to say hello and see how he was doing. He never expected this. "This is kind of a shock, Laura. I mean, I had no idea that – "

"I know. But I thought that the best way to show you that I could change was to just do it. So – here I am!"

He laughed. The absurdity of the week was getting to him. "Here you are."

She scooted closer. "I just think that what we had was too special to throw away. I am *so* sorry about everything that happened and…I'm not going to give up until you give me a second chance."

Matthew sat back. "I…don't know what to say."

"Don't say anything!" she said. "Just think it over."

He smiled, then rubbed his face with his hands. He felt tired – worn out from the week.

But he couldn't lie to himself – it was nice to see a familiar face, even if it wasn't someone he expected. Laura knew him, at least.

And still loved him, apparently.

He was about to open his mouth to speak again when Laura leaned forward and planted a kiss.

Matthew froze at first – somehow he didn't expect it. Mainly because he didn't expect *any* of this.

After a moment, he pulled away. "How about we...just take it slow?"

She smiled. "Sure. We can get to know each other again. What's the harm in that?"

Matthew couldn't think of a good response, so he settled with, "Alright."

They ended up talking and catching up into the late hours of the morning; it got so late that Matthew let her sleep in his bed while he took the couch.

Then they spent the entire day together on Sunday. It was awkward at first, but the feeling didn't last long. It felt like they picked up just where they left off.

Matthew was surprised by how natural it felt; he was strangely put at ease with her. The loneliness that had nagged him since he moved to the island was quieted; and for a moment, he just felt happy. It wasn't until now that he realized he'd isolated himself – perhaps too much.

The day was going well until Laura managed to get herself invited to Sunday dinner. It wasn't that he didn't want her to be there, it just seemed so fast. And then when she got there, she told everyone that she was his girlfriend.

That was *not* his favorite part of the weekend – they hadn't really discussed it. Or had they? He agreed to give her a second chance, but he didn't realize that it meant they'd jump right back in. At the same time, it sort of made sense?

He wasn't sure. His plan was to see where it went; there was no harm in trying. And it wasn't like he had any luck dating on the island. He wasn't as charming as Luke – he wasn't charming at all, actually. And so far, all he'd managed to do was scare the daylights out of the only girl he had feelings for – Jade. That was the second time she'd turned him down – he needed to take the hint.

On Monday morning, he went into work to talk to Chief about Jade's case.

"I think I'd like to question at least a few people to make sure they weren't responsible. Just to see how they respond."

Chief nodded. "Alright. Who were you thinking?"

"Well, her ex-husband for starters. Someone named Barb – she made a vague threat towards Jade."

"Barb? Barb McFarland?" He made a face as though he were thinking. "Yeah – I could see it. Maybe."

"And it might be a bit of a stretch, but Brock or Andrea? They could be trying to get back at Morgan."

"Yeah…it's possible. But let's hold off on that for now and check the others first."

Matthew nodded. "Sounds like a plan to me."

He set out for Anacortes right away. As far as he knew, Brandon still worked at the grocery store in town. He got there just around noon and asked an employee about him.

"Is he in trouble?" the woman asked, eyes wide.

Matthew smiled. "I don't think so – unless you know something that I don't?"

Brandon appeared a few moments later.

"Hey man," he said, putting his hands up. "I don't want any trouble."

Matthew crossed his arms and leaned back. "Nor do I. How have you been, Brandon?"

"Fine. Okay. Why?"

"When's the last time that you went to San Juan Island?"

"I don't go *anywhere* near that island," said Brandon. "I don't even take DJ jobs there. I told you, I don't want any trouble."

"That seems pretty drastic if you're not doing anything wrong."

Brandon shrugged. "You can check the ferry logs, or whatever it is that you do. I haven't been over there. Not at all."

Matthew nodded. Unlike the movies, there wasn't some high-tech system where he could see everyone who traveled on the ferry the last few months. It would be great technology to have, but it didn't exist. However, Brandon didn't seem to know that.

"I already checked."

"Then you know that I haven't been over there!"

"It's not the only way to get to the island." Matthew took a step forward. "So maybe you could tell me where you were on Wednesday."

"I was here!" Brandon said. "I worked from noon until close. You can ask anyone."

"Thanks, I will."

"What's this about?"

Matthew studied him for a moment. If his alibi were true, there was no way that he could have been the one to break into

Jade's house. Though he still could've sent one of his friends. "It's about your ex-wife."

"Okay?"

"Someone broke into her house."

Brandon's mouth dropped open. "I swear I didn't have *anything* to do with that!"

"That's good."

He crossed his arms. "Is she okay?"

Matthew stared at him. He didn't look particularly threatening – especially in his forest green apron. "She is, thankfully. But if you know anything about it, I'd appreciate it if you came to me."

"I don't know anything, but yeah – I would. Tell you, I mean."

Matthew nodded. This conversation was going nowhere. "Thanks Brandon. You take care – I'll be keeping an eye on you."

Brandon frowned. "Thanks."

Matthew spoke to a manager to confirm Brandon's whereabouts and his story checked out. He wasn't completely convinced that Brandon was innocent, but he didn't have any alarm bells going off either. The guy seemed clueless – hapless even. Jade also didn't think that he was involved – and she should know what he was capable of, right?

When Matthew got back to the island, he attempted to interview Barb as well, but she was nowhere to be found. First he went to her restaurant, but none of her employees knew where she was. He then went to her house, but there was no answer. He'd have to track her down another time.

The rest of his shift was uneventful, and on Tuesday he got pulled into patrol and wasn't able to work on Jade's case at all.

On Wednesday, he had the day off. He debated what to do with his evening. Laura suggested that she could make dinner for him. But he'd planned to go to the committee meeting at Jade and Morgan's and didn't want to let them down.

Ultimately, he decided to go to the committee meeting. He could have dinner with Laura any night. He called her to let her know his plans.

"Maybe we could do Saturday night instead?" he suggested.

"Oh! That'd be great. I was thinking that we could go and do some shopping?"

Matthew closed his eyes. He didn't want to groan, but at the same time...he didn't want to spend his weekend shopping either. "What do you need? I thought you had all of your furniture."

"I do, but I feel like I need to get a new plate set. The one I have isn't really working in this apartment."

"Ah. Are you going to go to the place with the fifty dollar plates?"

She laughed. "They're not *all* fifty dollars. But of course, it needs to be bone china!"

He didn't know what that meant, so he just said, "Right."

"Oh come on, it'll be fun! It'll be like old times. Oh – and I can tell you about the country club that I'm thinking of joining. You should join too! They have all kinds of events and we could do some golfing..."

"I don't really golf anymore," he said. It was something he'd always done with Laura's father in an attempt at bonding. It never went well.

"But you still have your clubs, right?"

"Nope. I sold them."

Laura gasped. "But I bought some of those for you! How could you just sell them?"

"I'm sorry – I just don't really like golfing."

"You love golfing! And you were so good – we can get you new ones. Anyway, how about you catch the early ferry on Saturday and we can have all day together?"

"Oh – okay. I can do that."

"Awesome! Can't wait!"

"Me too. Talk to you later."

As he was getting ready to go to Jade's place, he felt a bit guilty, imagining Laura at home by herself. He pushed it out of his mind though – he could make it up to her when they went plate shopping for four hours that weekend.

He got to Jade's house a few minutes late because Toast refused to come inside after his potty break. When he knocked on the door, Jade answered.

"Oh!" she said. "Matthew! I didn't know that you were coming – I'm sorry, we already got started."

"No, I'm sorry – I should've texted. But I figured that once I was part of the committee, it's a lifelong term."

She laughed and stepped aside to let him in. "It's not lifelong. It's all voluntary."

"Don't believe her!" yelled Morgan. "She's working us to death."

"I am not!" Jade put her hands on her hips. "I've just been really busy the last week so there's a lot to do."

"What's going on?" asked Matthew as he took a seat on the couch. There was some sort of crumbly cake on the coffee table – blueberry? The smell pulled him in. Next to that was a plate of cookies.

"Well," Morgan took a deep breath. "Jade set a date for the fundraiser at her mom's barn – a perfectly reasonable two weeks from now."

Jade held up a finger. "Two and a *half* weeks, thank you."

"Oh, that's kind of soon," said Matthew. "But I'm sure we can make it work."

"Dear Jade, *why* is it so soon?" asked Luke. "Did you lose your calendar when you were booking it? Or did you just forget what month you were living in?"

"I didn't intend for it to work out like this," said Jade. "But when I looked at the dates that my mom had open, the dates the caterer was available, and any dates that wouldn't compete with already planned events on the island...this was the only one."

"Right – so it'll be fine. It's all going to be fine," said Morgan.

Jade laughed. "If this is too much pressure, you can take a timeout and have a cookie."

"I will eat my cookies while I work, thank you." Morgan flopped onto the couch, a cookie in one hand and a laptop in the other.

"What can I do?" asked Matthew. "I need to earn my snacks too."

"I don't want to make you do anything," said Jade. "You shouldn't feel like you *have to* be part of this committee."

Oh shoot – was Jade trying to push him out because he'd made her feel uncomfortable? Should he say something about his botched kiss? Or would that just make it worse?

She hadn't said anything...but when he tried to kiss her, she'd made it perfectly clear that she immediately wanted to get away from him. He got the message loud and clear.

"No – I want to help, if you'll have me. I think it's a great idea, and I want to be a part of it."

A smile spread across her face – a genuine smile. "Really?"

"Yes, really! Please put me to work."

"Okay!" Jade sat next to Morgan. "But listen, Corporal. There's no backing out now."

Chapter 7

By the next weekend, Jade needed a break from planning her fundraiser and was excited by the chance to see what Burke Development put together for *their* event. Just before she got ready, she decided to spend a little time cleaning up the kitchen.

"So don't get mad at me," said Morgan as she popped her head into the room.

"Why?" Jade said slowly.

"I kind of, sort of, think I'll be a little bit late to the event today."

Jade frowned. "Why, what's going on?"

"I'm really sorry, but this client got back to me and the only time that she can meet is right at five. I'm hoping it won't take too long and I can still make it at some point."

"Oh. That's okay. Don't worry about it."

Jade didn't want Morgan to feel guilty; she'd already dedicated a lot of time to their plan for Colby Farm, and the entire committee didn't need to go to this party.

Jade wasn't even sure if *she* should go. The developers who wanted to buy the land invited the entire county to the event in Friday Harbor. When Jade initially told everyone about it at the committee meeting on Wednesday, Morgan and Matthew both volunteered to go and they made plans to scope it out.

Now it'd just be her and Matthew.

Jade frowned.

"Don't look so sad!" Morgan pleaded. "I promise that I'll get there as soon as I can."

"Oh – it's not that. It's not your fault at all. I understand."

Morgan crossed her arms. "Then what's wrong?"

"Nothing," Jade said, raising her voice a bit too high-pitched.

"Come on, I'm really sorry!"

Jade shook her head. "I swear, it's fine! I'll see you there later?"

Morgan studied her for a moment before responding. "Yeah, definitely. I'm sure they won't even know who you are."

"I didn't even think of that."

"Unless..." Morgan tapped her chin. "What if they're the ones who've been terrorizing you all this time?"

Jade laughed. "I don't think so. Nothing else has happened. I think Matthew was right – someone broke into the car and tried to get a two-for-one deal with the garage door opener. We're probably fine now."

"Maybe. But hey, at least Matthew can go!"

Jade nodded. "Yeah."

"Hopefully he doesn't try to bring his girlfriend. I don't buy her 'I'm so cute and everyone's my friend' routine at all."

"*Morgan*!" Jade said sternly. "She seems nice. We can't be mean to her because..."

"Because what?"

Jade sighed. She might as well come out and say it. "Because I thought that Matthew might like me."

"I think he *does* like you. Just because – "

"No, stop. I'm not doing this," Jade said. "I will go to the party with him, and if Laura is there, I'm sure she'll be a nice addition. And when you come, you'll be nice to her and we'll be one big, happy family!"

"Speak for yourself!" Morgan replied with a smirk. "I don't have to be nice to anyone."

Jade laughed. "You're right, what was I thinking?"

She decided that she wasn't going to change any of her plans just because Morgan couldn't make it. She wanted to get there early, take a look around, and leave. Simple.

She'd see Matthew whenever he got there. And if he didn't come, that was fine too. Jade knew how to blend into a crowd.

Just before five, she made her way towards Friday Harbor. The event was being held at the Brickworks Event Center, and she didn't want to have a hard time finding parking. Unfortunately, despite thinking that she was planning ahead, there was almost no parking by the time she got there. It looked like the entire island was coming to this thing.

They were officially calling it "A Meet and Greet with Burke Development." Jade scoffed. What a ridiculous name for an event that was clearly just an advertisement for their business.

It took her almost ten minutes to find a parking spot; when she finally found a place, she wasn't even sure if it was legal. She made sure that she wasn't blocking anything important before locking her car; if she were breaking any laws, surely her step-dad would be able to help? The thought of it made her laugh – asking Chief Hank to get her out of a parking ticket.

Would he really help her? She couldn't decide, but hoped she wouldn't have to find out.

As Jade approached the building, she paused to survey how many people were coming to this event. The building itself was stuffed with people; partygoers spilled outside onto the romantically lit patio, which was dotted with heaters. There was even an outdoor bar!

How irritating. And everyone looked so happy. Why were they so impressed by this? Just because this company had money? What was so great about that!

She let out a huff before delicately weaving through the crowd to get into the building. As she got closer, the music grew louder and louder; it wasn't until she was inside that she realized it was coming from a live band. Some people were dancing; others were milling about and chatting with cocktails and drinks.

A waiter approached. "May I interest you in a glass of champagne, miss?"

Champagne? That was overkill.

"No thank you," she said firmly. Just because she was there didn't mean that she needed to be charmed by these...con artists.

A man behind her asked her to move, then reached past her to grab a glass of champagne. Jade decided to investigate a video that was being projected onto one of the walls – when she got close enough she could mostly make out the audio.

"Burke Development, a subsidiary of Burke Industries, specializes in a luxury experience..."

The video panned across a white sand beach and a bright blue, glistening pool. Did these idiots have any idea what kind of island this was? Did they know the difference between the Pacific Ocean and Bermuda?

"Hey there," said a voice behind her.

She spun around. "Oh! Hey Matthew."

"So how much does this video make you want to win the vote?"

Jade looked around to make sure that no one was listening to them. "Only about a hundred times more than before I walked in here."

He laughed. "I mean, I get what they're trying to sell here. But it looks so generic, doesn't it? It doesn't seem to fit San Juan."

"*Exactly!* It doesn't fit at *all*. Even the video just looks like stock footage. What do they plan to build here? Are they going to try to install a man-made white sand beach that can never be used because the water is too cold?"

He shook his head. "I don't know. They keep advertising their luxury hotel line, but that seems like a bad fit too."

Jade sighed. "Yeah. I'm not sure what they're doing. And they're not really supplying that information, are they?"

"Not that people seem to care."

"I know." Jade looked around the room; maybe people just came for the free food and alcohol?

Another waiter stopped. "Champagne?"

"Yes, thank you," said Matthew, reaching out and taking two glasses.

Jade shot him a look.

He shrugged. "If they're paying."

She weighed that for a moment before deciding to take a glass as well.

"Darn it," she muttered after her first sip. "That's really good."

"Is it?" Matthew pulled away, making a face after finishing the first glass. "It tastes like sugary bubbles."

"Well you don't have to drink it!" she said with a laugh.

"No, if it's good then it was probably expensive. I need to do my part to destabilize their operation." He drained the second glass before setting it down on a nearby table.

Jade smiled to herself. Perhaps not the most effective way to fight them, but he wasn't wrong.

Someone bumped into Jade's back, causing the champagne to slop out of her glass and onto the floor.

"I'm so sorry," the woman said as she spun around. When she recognized Jade, however, her facial expression deadened.

"It's okay Barb, I just need to find a way to wipe this up so no one slips on it..."

"Good luck with that," Barb said flatly.

Matthew took a step closer. "Barb? Barb McFarland?"

"Yes?"

"It's so nice to finally meet you, I'm Corporal Matthew Stevens." He extended his hand. "I've been trying to get in touch with you."

Jade watched Barb's expression carefully. Her mouth popped open before widening into a smile that spanned her face. "Oh, of course! Yes, my staff told me that you dropped by. I've been so busy with everything, I'm sorry I didn't manage to get back to you yet."

"Well I'm glad that we can connect now," Matthew responded. "Would you mind stepping over here for a moment?"

"Oh – of course not."

Jade watched, unable to make out what they were saying; their conversation was drowned out in the murmur of the crowd. But she still enjoyed watching Barb's animated face, the exaggerated use of her hands, and her wild gesticulations – which resulted in another spill of champagne. To see her go from an award winning death stare to this performance made the hassle of parking worth it.

Matthew, however, was unchanged. When he spoke to her, his face remained neutral – even kind at times. It seemed that Jade rarely got to see him in anything other than his Sheriff's uniform anymore, but he blended right in.

Well – except for being taller than almost everyone in the room. Jade guessed he must've been at least six foot four, maybe even six foot five. He was even taller than Luke, and much more muscular – which, naturally, resulted in constant nicknames from Luke ranging from the basic accusations of "you big, beautiful man" to the more specific "Corporal Clydesdale."

Matthew never really addressed these comments; he'd just laugh and shake his head. Never once had he made a comment about his own appearance; though he must work out, right? Probably a lot. Jade didn't know. Even now his muscles seemed to just barely fit inside the sleeves of his buttoned up shirt...

She forced herself to stop staring and instead look around the room for Laura. Luckily, she wasn't anywhere to be seen. Not that Jade didn't *want* Laura to be involved, but if she were here, that would force Jade to be the awkward third wheel.

When Jade turned back around, Matthew was now chatting with both Barb and a guy she didn't recognize. He was also tall – not as tall as Matthew, though, and a bit more gangly. He seemed out of place – he was wearing dress pants and a vest. Definitely more dressed up than anyone here. But then, he also had his sleeves rolled up.

"Jade!" Matthew yelled, waving her over.

Oh dear. She didn't want to be involved in this, but now they were all looking at her and smiling. Even Barb was fake smiling.

She had no choice. She walked over to them.

"Hi," she said with a small wave.

"Jade, I'd like you to meet Eric Burke. He's the developer in charge of this project."

Ah. So *that's* why he had his sleeves rolled up. He wanted to look like he was just "one of the guys." It was like what politicians did whenever they talked to anyone but their rich donors.

Jade extended a hand. "It's nice to meet you, I'm Jade Clifton."

"I know who you are!" he replied. "You're my competition!"

Jade let out a little laugh. "Well – I guess you could say that."

"Right, because *what* kind of competition will that even be?" Barb said sweetly. "Look at this! People *love* it Mr. Burke!"

Matthew and Jade locked eyes for a moment, but Jade had to look away so she wouldn't burst into laughter.

"You're too kind, and please, call me Eric." He turned towards Jade. "Are you enjoying the party?"

Jade nodded. "Yes – it's very beautiful. It seems like you got a great crowd."

"When's your party?" asked Barb. "Or is it a fundraiser, I'm not sure?"

Matthew cleared his throat. "It's both. And it's next week, actually. We expect a pretty exciting turnout."

Oh man, what was the point in lying? She appreciated Matthew's effort, but they had no idea who was going to show up. So far, all they managed to do was get onto the community Facebook page and print some flyers.

"That's wonderful! I wish I could make it," said Eric. "I love a lively community like this. Really gives you a warm feeling, doesn't it?"

Jade looked around. It was nice seeing everyone come together – even if it was for the competition. "It does."

"Well, I wish you the best of luck," Eric said, shaking their hands, "and I look forward to talking to you again, have fun!"

"Good luck with your party," said Barb flatly before disappearing into the crowd.

Jade looked up at Matthew. "I think we really have our work cut out for us."

He smiled as he popped a stuffed mushroom into his mouth. "Don't worry. I've already cost them half a bottle of champagne. And we haven't even gotten started yet."

"Right." Jade grabbed a bacon-wrapped pickle from a nearby platter. She expected it to be terrible, but of course, it was delicious. "We've got a good team, don't we?"

"The best." He smiled. "They don't stand a chance."

Chapter 8

On the morning of Jade's fundraiser, Margie woke up before her alarm; she was too nervous and excited to sleep. She crept out of bed, leaving Hank snoring in his normal way. She didn't know why she was trying to be quiet – even with literal hammering on the walls, he wouldn't wake up. It was a good thing, most of the time, and especially today.

She got dressed, ate a piece of toast, and filled her travel mug with coffee before hopping into her car. Her first stop was the trolley company. The owner owed her a favor for a wedding last year, and Margie called it in for Jade's fundraising party. She negotiated a *very* fair rate to transport guests to the barn – they even planned to pick people up in town and along the way.

It was one small way for Margie to contribute. Poor Jade was so worried that no one was going to show up, especially after seeing the party that Burke Development pulled off. Margie was determined to help in every way possible.

Everything was set for the trolleys, so her next stop was at the caterer. It was a company that often did weddings at the barn – Mary's Bistro Catering – and they, too, were excited by the idea of Colby Smith's land actually being used for the people of San Juan; they offered their food and services almost at cost for the event. Margie stopped by to drop off some containers that they'd forgotten at the barn a few weeks prior and Mary assured her that everything was on track. She even had plans for extra cold food in case more people showed up than originally expected.

Margie was satisfied with that and went back home to finish up some baking; she knew that Mary had desserts planned, but she wanted to be sure that there was no chance of running out.

The day prior, she spent about ten hours baking cakes, cookies, and four separate pies. Today she just had a few dozen more cookies planned – nothing major. She'd also ordered small, custom printed paper bags from one of her friends on the island. They read "Vote YES on Proposition 16 – Colby's Farm!" The idea was for the party guests to fill them with cookies and treats – and hopefully, remember how to vote when the time came.

Once the cookies were cooling, she went out to the barn to help with setup. It'd been a while since she was so involved in an event, and she was loving every minute of it. It was energizing – and she wanted to make everything as perfect for Jade as possible. She cared about the project too, of course. But not as much as Jade seemed to care about it. She was spending almost all of her free time working on this and whatever was important to Jade was important to Margie.

The barn was bustling with activity. Jade was there setting up tables and decorations; Luke and Hank were positioning a large TV in the corner of the barn as Morgan tried to connect her laptop to it.

"Mom!" Jade hugged her when she arrived. "Chief Hank told me you've been running around all morning!"

"Isn't he observant?" Margie said with a smile. "Don't worry – the trolleys and food are all set. And I have a surprise for you."

She pulled out one of the paper bags and handed it over; there were even a few of Jade's favorite cookies inside for effect.

"This is *so* nice! Where did you get these?"

"I have my secrets," she said with a smile. "Do you like it?"

"Yes, it's adorable!"

"And I've made a few dozen extra cookies so there should be plenty to fill them with at the end of the night."

Jade's jaw dropped. "You didn't have to do all of this. You've got to be exhausted, Mom."

"I'm not some old lady who has to be kept inside," Margie said. "It's one thing if you don't like it – you can tell me, but if you – "

"I never called you an old lady," Jade said, placing a hand on her shoulder. "And I love it, really. You're the best, Mom."

Margie smiled. "Good. I try. Okay, I'm going to get back to work. Let me know if you need anything."

"Okay!"

It was nice to see Jade so excited. Margie didn't have time to dawdle, though; she needed to finish setting up her center-pieces. She made them herself – some of the flowers were from the florist, but others were from her own garden. She wanted to make sure that there was a San Juan Island touch; she included sprigs of lavender and sand in the vases. They might not be able to outspend Eric Burke, but they had other charms.

Over the next hour and a half, they got the video running on the TV and also made a few last-minute changes to loca-tions of the hors d'oeuvres and dessert tables. At one point, Morgan had to practically drag Jade away so she would have time to get ready.

"You'd better get ready too, Margie!" Morgan called out. "When I get back here I expect you to have your hostess dress on."

Margie laughed. "It'll take me no time at all to get ready."

Which was good, because they almost had no time left. She rushed back into the house and ran into Hank when she walked in the door.

"There you are, stranger," he said, wrapping her in a hug.

"Hi honey! I can't talk, I have to get ready and go back so I can tell the caterers – "

"You have to boss the caterers around?" He tightened his grip. "You know, we never get to have quality time together anymore. You've been so busy. You're not busy now, are you?"

Margie laughed and stopped struggling against him. It was no use – he was too strong. And too determined. "I know, I know. How about we have some quality time together *at* the fundraiser?"

He looked up as though he was seriously considering it. "Okay. Deal."

She got up on her tiptoes and kissed him on the cheek. "Love you!"

"Love you too."

Margie showered and got dressed in a hurry. She didn't really care what she looked like, but she at least needed to have her hair dried; she threw on an old dress that she'd worn to Tiffany's graduation from college.

It still fit – mostly. It was a little tight. She studied herself in the mirror for a moment just to make sure that it didn't look absurd.

Nah. It would do.

After five minutes of putting on makeup, she decided that she'd done *more* than enough. It was time to get back to the barn.

They only had about half an hour before guests started to arrive, so Margie got busy with making sure that the catering staff was set up and that they knew what they were doing for the night. Amazingly, it seemed like they'd avoided any major disasters so far.

The first trolley load of guests arrived a few minutes after seven. There were only about fifteen people – two of them were friends from the sheriff's department, and the rest were related to friends Margie knew from her book club. Margie tried to keep Jade busy until the next trolley arrived – she didn't want her to get her spirits down.

Luckily, the second trolley brought about forty people, and a few cars pulled in to park as well.

"See!" She whispered as they watched them enter the barn. "You had nothing to worry about. They're practically *busting* down the doors!"

Jade smiled. "If we can even get half of what they had last weekend, I think I'll be happy."

Morgan and Luke were busy playing bartender to the new arrivals. Margie was about to rush off and make sure the appetizers were ready, but as soon as she walked into the barn, she could see that everything was laid out beautifully. What was left for her to do?

She rejoined Jade and introduced her to some friends who'd never gotten a chance to meet her in person – though Margie gushed about her constantly. She knew she was doing it, but sometimes she just couldn't stop herself.

They spent the next twenty minutes or so chatting with them, and then transitioned to a conversation with the guests whose kids were occupying the arts and crafts table.

That was one major thing that Jade wanted to be different about her party – she wanted whatever Colby's Farm turned into to ultimately be family-friendly, so she decided that the fundraiser should be, too.

Jade had to get creative to ensure that there were activities for all different age groups, but she was able to make a nice arrangement. Luckily, two ladies from Margie's book club volunteered to man the table; both of them had plenty of real world grandma experience and so far, they were doing great.

More and more guests poured in, and Jade's nervousness seemed to ease. She watched the door carefully, and at one point grabbed Margie's arm.

"Oh! Mom, do you see those three? Those are the county council members. I want to introduce you."

"If you insist!"

Jade led them across the barn where a large group was waiting in line for drinks.

"Hi guys, I'm *so glad* that you could make it!" Jade reached out and shook everyone's hand. "I'd like you all to meet my mom, Margie Clifton."

Margie waved. "Hi, and welcome!"

"This is the full council – Jared, Angie, and Frank."

Margie smiled. "It's nice to finally meet you all! I've heard so much about you – you're the ones who gave Jade a chance to come up with an idea for this land, so for that, I thank you!"

Jared, the youngest one of the bunch by several decades, touched his hand to his chest. "Oh, it was our pleasure. Really – a no-brainer."

Angie, a woman closer to Margie's age, nodded. "I was excited that Jade even wanted to take it on! The only other interest we had was from developers, of course. So what she's doing – what you're all doing – it's just wonderful!"

"I'm just here for the food," said Frank with a hearty laugh. "Just kidding. I like a good debate. It livens things up on the council, you know?"

"Oh I know," said Margie, smiling like the fool that she was, with no idea what he was talking about.

"No, this really is good," Frank continued. "I knew Colby. He didn't get involved a lot in island politics, but he was a good guy. He'd be really touched to see all this going on. Oh – excuse me, my granddaughter looks like she's about to jump off of that table."

Margie turned around and saw a four-year-old girl on top of the arts and crafts table, both fists in the air. She laughed to herself – it'd been a long time since she had to deal with problems like that.

"The whole island is really excited about it," said Jared. He then paused, his eyes narrowing at someone across the room. "Oh, there's someone I need to talk to – please excuse me."

Margie watched Jade as Jared walked away. Was it possible that Jade liked him? He wasn't a bad looking guy – not at all. And he looked like he was around Jade's age. He'd come dressed up in a suit and was very clean-cut. Maybe he and Jade had a sort of friendship going on? Or maybe...more than a friendship? Jade would never tell, but Morgan might spill the beans...

"Oh look," Jade said, dropping her voice. "Jared's talking to Eddie."

"Interesting." Margie hadn't seen Eddie since he *finally* finished up the work she paid him for in the barn. She never made the mistake of hiring him again – he was just too unreliable. "Looks like Eddie's trying to smooth talk him. I wonder what he did this time."

Jade giggled. "Who knows."

Margie decided to make her way over and find out for herself. But when she got closer, Jared was already walking away.

Margie decided to approach Eddie anyway. "Eddie! I'm surprised to see you here."

"An artist must always return to see his work," he said with a grin.

He'd only worked on the bathrooms, so it didn't quite seem like art to Margie. But if that's the way that he wanted to think of it?

"Yes, of course. How have you been?"

"Excellent! I really like what you've done with the place."

"Thank you." Margie cleared her throat. "Is my memory wrong, or did Jade tell me that you were *against* her proposal for the land? You said it would be bad for your business?"

He laughed, putting his arm around her. "Margie, that was then. This is now! I realize that no matter *what* they build on that land, I can help build it. You'll put in a good word for me, right?"

"I can let them know what you did here," she said carefully. She didn't want to lie to the man – she certainly would never recommend him to *anyone*.

"You're the best!"

Margie caught Hank's eyes from across the room. She had to force herself not to laugh – he was staring daggers at Eddie. He really didn't like the guy.

Eddie was babbling something in her ear, but she wasn't listening. At that moment, Matthew walked into the barn –

with Laura on his arm. She had on a long, yellow dress. It was quite stunning, really. Margie looked around to see where Jade was. It took her a moment to spot her – she seemed to be fully engaged in a conversation with some people near the TV.

Margie watched her carefully – she didn't seem to notice that Matthew was there at all, which was a relief. Jade never mentioned anything about Matthew, but Margie didn't need to ask her. She saw how Jade's expression changed the moment that Laura walked into that Sunday dinner.

Even if it was just a flash across her face, Margie knew what it meant. Jade looked like she'd been swatted down, and it broke Margie's heart.

Laura could be the nicest girl in the world and Margie would still dislike her. It didn't matter if it was silly – Jade was her daughter, and she'd always be on her side.

At least Jade was busy now. And it looked like the dessert table was getting a bit barren, so Margie ran to the kitchen to grab a few plates of her cookies. She *knew* they'd come in handy!

The rest of the evening flew by, with people coming in all the time. An hour before the end of the party, Jade caught her by the arm with breathless excitement.

"Mom, this is *incredible!* We've gotten donations from seventy-nine people. I know it doesn't sound like a lot, but a few people – I'm guessing who are pretty rich – donated a couple thousand dollars *each!* Can you believe that?"

"I *can* believe it, you have a great plan and the video that you have playing is really impressive! Do you know the total yet?"

"Yes! Just about twenty-six thousand dollars. Isn't that just *insane!*"

"That's wonderful honey!"

At the end of the evening, Jade got on the microphone and thanked everyone for coming. "I also have to thank my wonderful committee for all of their hard work so far. And of course, my lovely mom, Margie, who loaned us the use of the barn tonight."

Applause rippled across the barn.

"Don't forget to grab a bag of cookies for your trip home – the trolleys are lining up outside. Have a great night everyone!"

As the guests slowly filtered out, Margie went around the side of the barn; she wanted to run back home and grab the last of the paper bags so they wouldn't run out. Out of the corner of her eye, she saw what looked like movement and she froze.

She squinted into the darkness. "Hello?"

Margie approached the side of the barn to get a better look, but there didn't seem to be anyone there. She took out her cellphone and turned on the light – what she saw took her breath away. Spray-painted on the side were the words "GIVE UP BEFORE SOMEONE GETS HUR!!!"

Chapter 9

"Do you think that last word was supposed to be 'hurt'?" Laura asked with a frown.

"No," Morgan said evenly. "I think it was supposed to be 'hurry'. Like 'hurry up and remember how to spell,' because the person who did this is an idiot."

Jade covered her face with her hands and let out a sigh. This was not a good end to the evening. Thankfully, the guests were gone and no one else had seen the message.

"I just can't believe that someone would do this," Jade's mom said. "And how did we not see them!"

Chief Hank squatted down to get a closer look at the ground. "There was too much commotion. And you did see them – you scared them off. It doesn't seem like they left anything behind, though."

"Yeah, they were definitely cut short," Matthew said. "But then again – they managed to get the exclamation points in."

"Yes, they'd meant to have ten exclamation points actually, so we knew they meant business," Luke said. "Spelling wasn't a priority for them, though."

"I don't like this," her mom said. "I don't like that someone is making threats. Especially after everything that happened to you, Jade."

"It's a pretty lame threat." Jade stood with her arms crossed. "I am sorry about the barn though, Mom. I'll help you repaint it."

"I'm not worried about the barn," she replied. "I'm worried about you."

Jade shook her head. "Don't be worried. I'm not scared, and this isn't going to stop me."

Jade gave her mom a hug and told her they'd find a day to paint together. There wasn't much else to do, so slowly, everyone dispersed and went home.

She didn't want to worry her, but this whole situation was ridiculous. The only reason someone decided to spray paint the barn was because they could see that the fundraiser was a success.

Not only had they raised a bunch of money, they also had a ton of people show up and get excited for their plan! Throughout the course of the night, the party attracted at least a few hundred people. The earlier crowd came with kids, but later on a different crowd filtered in – a younger group that Jade thought would be hard to reach. But they came! And they were excited!

Somehow they managed not to run out of food – though it was close. And thanks to her mom's very dedicated baking, they didn't even come close to running out of desserts.

It was a huge success, and Jade refused to allow this coward to scare her. Not when they were finally making progress.

The rest of the week was packed with activities. On Monday, Jade took a break during her workday to go to the local news station. She'd tried reaching them by email, but never got a response. When she actually showed up at the station, she realized why – they didn't exactly have a ton of people running the operation.

She spoke to someone named Cindy who was quite nice and very happy to air their video for Proposition 16. Jade also managed to get a link to the video on the county website – so if anyone was looking for more information about the vote, they would find it right away.

On her way home, Jade stopped by her mom's house to say hello, but there was no answer when she knocked on the door. It was disappointing, but she didn't want to bug her mom – maybe she was buying supplies to repaint the barn?

Jade went home and finished creating a fundraising website for their project that she'd been working on. On Tuesday, she took a half day from work so she could go to Orcas and Lopez Islands to spread the word about the project; she wanted to get some opinions from the residents there as well, and she was excited to see that more than fifty people came to each event.

It was important to get as many opinions as possible. She spoke to someone from the parks department at the fundraiser, and he said that if the county got to keep the land, they could turn it into another park. They had a little bit of money in the budget for some new development, and he said that they could also apply for a grant to build something.

She was open to any and all possibilities. She couldn't believe how much they'd raised already – but at the same time, she knew that actually getting something built would cost a lot more than twenty-six thousand dollars.

On Wednesday, the committee met – minus Matthew – and went over the wording for the ballot. Angie recommended that they include a section in the proposition that said it wouldn't cost the taxpayers anything to have this land remain in control of the county.

"But that's not really true, is it?" asked Jade. "Because if we do build something here – like a park or some sort of a recreation center – won't the county have to maintain it?"

Morgan waved a hand. "Don't worry about that. All people care about is that their taxes aren't going to go up."

"It's not like we're proposing a tax increase."

"Exactly. And don't make this too long, or no one's going to read it."

"True," said Jade. "It seems like everyone that I talked to is really excited about it, though."

"Sure. But think of the people who will just show up on voting day and not even know about it. I think we need to write it for them."

Luke agreed. "She's right, you know. I've had to explain this to my roommates like three times and they still don't really get it."

Jade laughed. "Good point."

It would've been nice to have Matthew's help on this, but he had some excuse as to why he couldn't come to the meeting; he said that he had to work. But was that even true? Maybe he was sick of wasting his evenings on this project and wanted to spend time with someone else...like Laura.

Maybe he felt like he couldn't bring Laura around. She did come to some things – like the fundraiser. Though throughout the whole evening, they didn't talk much and when they did, Jade felt nervous because Morgan wavered between completely ignoring Laura and being openly hostile.

Jade begged her to just act normally, explaining that she didn't want to lose Matthew as a friend. All Morgan had to say about that was, "He doesn't deserve to have you as a friend!"

Eventually, Morgan settled on at least looking in Laura's direction when she spoke. She still didn't really respond to Laura, but that was probably for the best; it was certainly better than her making snarky comments. That was the best she could do and Jade could only hope that Laura didn't feel unwelcome.

Morgan was definitely angrier at Matthew than Jade was. Jade wasn't angry at all – mostly she found the entire thing embarrassing. Seeing Laura more often made it worse, too. Laura was a beautiful woman, so put together and so...unlike Jade.

Laura and Matthew were a great pair – but it made it even more obvious that Matthew couldn't possibly have had any feelings for her.

She just wished that Morgan would drop it. What if Matthew caught wind of it? He'd think she was so...pathetic. If he didn't already, with her paranoia and her crazy ex-husband.

At least the project gave her something else to focus on. And she was appreciative of Matthew's help – whatever he could offer.

The meeting went well and by Friday night, Jade was spent. Morgan and Luke had to go to the mainland for a two day shoot, so Jade had the house to herself. She considered bringing dinner over to her mom, but she was so tired that all she could manage was to microwave a frozen burrito and watch half of a romance movie on TV.

By nine, she crawled into bed, rewarding her hard week of work with an early bedtime.

Chapter 10

The last light in the house went out.

Huh. That was easy.

When he'd gotten to the house and saw that someone was inside, he thought he'd have to hide in the backyard for hours before they went to sleep. It was a Friday night after all, but apparently this girl didn't have an active social life.

She was a strange girl, this Jade. No wonder she had so much time to harp on and on about Proposition 16. The girl lived like a grandma. She was always home. Never went out, never even went to work. Didn't have a boyfriend – nothing. At least the other girl that lived there – the loud one – left every once in a while. The only time granny Jade went out was to cause trouble about the vote.

Whatever, it didn't matter. If she wanted to go to bed early, then it made life a lot easier for him. He was supposed to step it up – increase the pressure on her. Turn up the heat.

Nothing he'd done so far worked in scaring her, and people were starting to get angry. Was this girl stupid or something? Was she not connecting the dots? Or did she just not care?

There was no way to tell. But the message he'd left at the barn wasn't enough. A normal person would've stopped – a normal person wouldn't have gone to the news to get their video on TV.

This Jade obviously wasn't normal, though. Not right in the head. That's how all of these young kids were – they thought they were invincible. Thought they should do something to change the world, even when they had no idea how the real world worked.

He looked around to make sure that nobody was watching. It was completely dark and it didn't seem like there was another soul within earshot. Even the street was quiet – no cars. This was a nice little neighborhood. No wonder these girls felt safe living here. It wouldn't take much to wake them up.

He had a pretty good plan that wouldn't leave behind any evidence. Not that the police could piece anything together – they hadn't so far.

He opened up the bundle of firewood that he'd brought and untied it, hoping that the logs wouldn't make too much noise as they settled onto the ground; they didn't cooperate, though, clumsily and loudly falling in all directions.

For a moment he paused – had anyone heard?

Didn't seem like it.

Carefully, he picked up a few pieces and laid them out in the shape of an S. Next was the T, then the letter O, and finally the P.

It didn't have to be as long as the message at the barn – thankfully. She should know what "STOP" meant by now. For effect, he added two exclamation points, using piles of dry leaves to serve as the dots.

He stood back for a moment and admired his work – it was big, at least four feet tall and five feet across – and it would send a big message. Right next to her window, too. It'd be perfect, maybe even wake her up.

Hopefully this would be the last thing he had to do. He looked around one more time to make sure that no one was watching before squatting down and holding a match to the S.

The tip of the wood caught on fire for a moment before fizzling out. He tried three more times with the same result.

"You've got to be kidding me," he muttered.

Luckily, he'd brought some lighter fluid along as a backup plan. He squirted some of it onto the S, then decided that all of the letters could use some – just to get them started. He ended up emptying the entire bottle – better safe than sorry. He couldn't have any of his fingerprints left behind on the wood or something. That would be bad.

He stood up, this time lighting a match and tossing it onto the wood. Finally, the stupid S caught on fire. The flames moved slowly but surely towards the T.

But maddeningly, the T was an inch too far away to catch the flames. He squatted down to push them together.

Finally, the T caught fire...but so did the bottom of his pants. He must've spilled some of the lighter fluid, because the flame was moving fast.

He resisted the urge to scream and smothered the small flame by kicking his leg into the grass in front of him, knocking the O slightly.

Within seconds, all of the wood was completely inflamed – including the parts of the O which were kicked into a nearby shrub.

It happened in an instant – the dry shrub absorbed the flame, almost coaxing it, all the way up the parched branches.

"Not good!" He looked around. There was still no one to be seen, and he didn't have any way to put out the flames that had spread, engulfing the shrub and licking the side of the house. He stepped back, shielding his eyes from the smoke.

It was moving hot and it was moving fast. Panicked, he took one last look around before running back to his car.

Chapter 11

It was a calm evening on San Juan Island. Matthew had an uneventful night, which was unusual for a Friday. There normally at least one person doing something stupid enough to warrant his attention.

But not tonight, it seemed. He drove around Friday Harbor a few times before he found himself on the street where Jade lived. He wasn't sure what possessed him to wander in that direction; he had no reason to be there.

Well actually – that wasn't completely true. Jade was threatened, blatantly, at the fundraiser. Matthew would've felt better if he could've stayed behind that night to thoroughly search the area, but it was impossible. Laura was impatient to leave and kept repeating how cold she was. Plus, Jade insisted that it didn't matter and no threat would stop her. She was quite stoic – it was jarring.

Matthew finally gave up and agreed to leave with Laura when he realized that a search would be futile – it wasn't like they could see much in the dark and all of the witnesses had already left.

She'd waited until they were driving home to start on him.

"I'm sure the police chief that *lives there* can figure it out," she said, arms crossed. "I don't know why you always have to be the one to save the world. Isn't it enough that you're a cop?"

"Well..."

"Oh, so you're going to have an attitude about it." She rifled through her purse, forcefully throwing lipstick and gum onto the floor. "I'm just trying to understand why you so desperately need to be a cop. And all the way out here! I mean, it's not even like things happen on this island. That spray paint looked like it was done by a ten year old. Is that really what you're here for Matthew?"

He let out a sigh. "Yes, because things like that matter. This might be the third threat against Jade. I don't want anything to happen to her."

Laura narrowed her eyes. "Oh? Would you say she's a *close* friend?"

"Come on Laura, don't attack me for answering your question. She's my boss's stepdaughter. And yes – she's a friend."

After a moment, she responded in a small voice. "I'm sorry. I didn't mean that. I'm just...having a hard time. Moving out here, living by myself. I don't have any friends. I feel isolated."

He glanced over at her. She'd stopped thrashing around in her purse, which was good, but she was sort of slumped over.

"It's okay," he said. "I'm sorry you feel that way. I wish you would get to know them – they're all really nice."

She nodded. "I will."

He looked over at the empty seat next to him now. Laura would've been quite bored with how he'd spent his Friday evening. And she'd be even *more* upset if she saw where he was now.

Matthew stopped his car on the street, two houses down from Jade's place. Laura would never say *why* she didn't like it, but it'd spark the same kind of argument that went nowhere.

There was no reason for her to be jealous, though. She asked for a second chance, and they were trying their best. He was definitely trying, and it wasn't easy.

The plate shopping, despite lasting five hours, was fine – that was something that he was used to. They didn't have their first real fight until she made him go to that country club. They went on the morning before the fundraiser, and the ensuing fight continued for the rest of the day.

The people were okay – not the friendliest, but whatever. Matthew's biggest issue with the whole idea was that a membership cost almost ten thousand dollars a year.

"Laura, how much money do you think I make?"

"It's not about the money, Matthew, it's about you valuing what's important to me. I want to be a part of this community, I want to fit in somewhere."

He sighed. "Can't we find a community to fit into that costs less?"

Through hours of arguing, he found out that the answer to that question was no. At least from her perspective.

The fight was so bad that they ended up being an hour late to Jade's fundraiser. At one point, Matthew came close to just leaving and going without her, but she didn't like the idea of that, and ultimately got in the car.

He shook his head, trying to put that entire night out of his mind. Instead he studied Jade's house; it looked like the lights were off. Maybe she wasn't even home? Her car was outside, though. What if she was out on a date or something and then came home to find him sitting out there like a creep?

He didn't want to make it awkward. She probably already thought that he was a creep, though she'd never said anything – thankfully. But she may have told Morgan about his unwanted kiss attempt.

Of course she told Morgan – why wouldn't she? But at the same time, that seemed like something that Morgan wouldn't be able to keep to herself. And if Morgan said something, even jokingly, in front of Laura...yikes. Laura wouldn't wait until they got to the car to start asking questions.

It hadn't happened yet, though. And Jade didn't seem like a girl who would kiss and tell.

The radio crackled alive. "217, dispatch."

Matthew cleared his throat. "217, go ahead."

"11-82. Spring and Mullis Street."

He let out a sigh. Not the most exciting call – just a traffic accident. No injuries, thankfully. And he couldn't sit outside of Jade's house all night. "217 en route."

He started the car and slowly rolled past Jade's house. He shot one more look – just a peek, just to make sure that nothing was out of place. And to make sure that she wasn't sitting there watching him. It didn't look like she was. Except...what was that?

There seemed to be smoke rising from the back of the house.

He didn't remember seeing a fire pit in the back yard... there was a grill, though. She could just be making some dinner. Or sitting out there with friends and a makeshift fire.

Matthew slowed down, straining to see what was going on. He couldn't go barging in on her like a stalker. But then again... it gave him a bad feeling.

He put the car into park. The accident could wait. The smoke was at least worth investigating. If she was back there and he caught her off guard, he could say that someone called in worried about the smoke.

No – he couldn't lie to her. He'd have to tell her the truth – that he was driving by and saw smoke. And when the guys at the station heard about it, they'd never stop making fun of him, especially if Jade was just having a bonfire. He could already envision it – they'd start calling him Smokey the Bear. He'd simply have to quit his job and move away from the island forever out of embarrassment.

He got out of the car and took a few long strides around the side of the house. There was a warm glow coming from the back yard – in all likelihood, a bonfire. He could stop by and say hello – it was probably just Morgan and Luke anyway.

As soon as he turned the corner, he saw it – a *massive* fire with flames spanning half of the house and reaching the roof. He stood stunned for a moment, just staring at it.

Matthew was about to reach a hand to his radio when he heard a scream ring out from inside the house.

Chapter 12

The beeping from the smoke detector roused Jade from sleep – but just barely. She flipped over, instinctively pulling a pillow over her head to drown out the noise. She'd always been a heavy sleeper, and it took a few moments before she realized that she needed to investigate the sound.

She rubbed her eyes, fumbling in the dark to turn on her bedside lamp. The lamp made a click, but the light wasn't working. It was still dark. She yawned and sat up in bed.

The air that she sucked in with her yawn burned her throat and made her cough. Her brain caught up in an instant – it wasn't that the light was broken, but that her room was filled with dark smoke.

Jade launched out of bed, coughing and stumbling towards the door. Just as she was about to reach it, part of the ceiling collapsed in front of her. She didn't realize that she was falling backward – she didn't know that she was screaming. Her head slammed into the corner of the bed as she landed on her side.

She didn't lose consciousness – instead it seemed that the pain woke her up even more. It was becoming harder and harder to breathe and the smoke was now so thick that she could hardly tell where she was or which direction she needed to go. Jade lowered herself to the ground, trying to crawl towards what she thought was the door.

A voice boomed from the hallway. "Jade!"

She tried to yell back, but all she managed was more coughing. How would they know where to find her if she couldn't respond?

That moment, her bedroom door flung open, a narrow beam of light piercing the smoke.

"Hang on, I'm going to get you out of here."

In a swift motion, Jade was scooped off of the floor and out of the room. Even just by getting to the living room, the air was clearer and she was finally able to take a breath. Within seconds, they were outside of the house and onto the street, the sound of sirens echoing in the distance.

Matthew gently set her down and took her face in his hands.

"You're okay, you're going to be okay," he repeated. "The ambulance will be here soon. Is there anyone else in the house?"

Jade shook her head, unable to speak. For every few breaths she took, she was forced into a coughing fit.

"It's okay, don't worry. I've got you."

He sat with her until she was finally able to take a few deep breaths. Jade looked back at the house – from the front, it hardly looked like anything was even wrong. It was eerily quiet on the street.

She looked back at Matthew. "Are you okay?"

He laughed. "Yeah – I'm fine. Are *you* okay?"

"Yeah. I'm fine now. I woke up and it was so smoky..."

"I know," he said. He brushed a strand of hair away from her face. "You're bleeding."

Jade absentmindedly darted a hand to her head and winced when she felt the gash. "Oh. The ceiling collapsed and I hit my head trying to get away. Does it look bad?"

He pulled away slightly, looking her over. "No. They'll fix you right up."

Jade couldn't tear her eyes away from him. He was so close and the world felt frozen around them. She had the urge to wrap her arms around his neck and bury her face in his shoulder.

She resisted that, though, and instead stared at him, studying the lines in his face, the gentle swoop of his hair. How did he manage to walk out of a fire looking so perfect?

"The paramedics are here. How about you let them check you out?" he said softly.

She nodded and tried to stand up, but stumbled.

"Let me help you," he said, stooping down so that she could reach her arm around his shoulders.

"Thanks." She steadied herself, surprised by his effortless power in supporting her. They slowly made their way to the ambulance.

Jade had no idea how long she was with the paramedics. She did her best to try to answer their questions while watching Matthew out of the corner of her eye; it wasn't long before he took off with the firefighters. An odd thought floated through her head – she realized Morgan's planning board for Colby Farm was in her room. Now they would have to make another one.

The paramedics recommended that she go to the emergency room to be checked out fully. She agreed to it – or she must've, because the next thing she knew, they were driving to the hospital. She felt a bit panicked when she realized that Matthew was still back at the house.

"Can you make sure that he doesn't go back in? That Matthew doesn't get hurt?"

The paramedic smiled. "Don't worry – he'll be just fine. Do you want us to call anyone to meet you at the hospital?"

"Oh yes – please. Could you call my mom?"

"Sure. What's her number?"

Jade opened her mouth and then closed it again. "I...can't remember. But I *know* her number. I just..."

"It's okay. You're probably still in shock."

"Her name is Margie. She's married to Chief Hank. Do you know Chief Hank?"

He laughed. "Of course, everyone knows Chief. Don't worry, we'll get in contact with them."

"Thank you. Oh – but can you please let my mom know that I'm okay? She'll have a heart attack when she gets a call from you."

When Jade got to the hospital, she started to feel a bit more with it. She still couldn't believe what had happened – and how quickly it all happened. But she was, at least, starting to wrap her head around the events.

A doctor came to see her within minutes of her arrival and ordered some blood work and testing. Jade had to sit in her room for a while after that, but a kind nurse gave her a warm blanket and some juice. It helped to sooth her throat.

After not too long, the doctor returned, closely followed by her mom.

"Oh my goodness, thank God that you're okay!"

She immediately went in for a hug, causing Jade to let out a little cough.

"I'm so sorry honey!"

Jade laughed. "I'm okay, really."

The doctor offered a handshake. "Hi, I'm Dr. Erron. Your daughter is going to be just fine."

"Thank you so much doctor."

Jade took a measured breath before speaking again. "Are my lungs okay?"

She nodded. "Yes, you're oxygenating fine and all of your testing was negative. You're going to have a nasty bump on your head, and you'll have to watch for any signs of a concussion, but I don't see any evidence of injury from smoke inhalation. It seems you got out just in the nick of time."

Her mom let out a whimper. "How could this happen?"

"I have no idea," Jade said, shaking her head. "I just woke up and my room was on fire."

Another whimper. "And you ran out of bed and out the door?"

Jade took a slow breath so as not to agitate her lungs. "Not exactly. I got disoriented. Then the ceiling collapsed – and that's when I hit my head. It was so dark in there..."

"How did you get out?"

Jade paused, wondering if she'd imagined it all. No – it was real.

He was real.

"Matthew ran in and picked me up."

Her voice cracked. Suddenly the gravity of it hit her. She almost died. If Matthew hadn't been there...

Her mom pulled her into another hug. "It's okay honey, you're safe now."

"Yeah," she said, clearing her throat. She still felt a little shaky and like she might burst into tears, but she was able to keep it together.

About an hour later, she got the okay to leave the hospital and Chief Hank came to pick them up.

"Hi," Jade said sheepishly as she got into the back of his police car. "Actually – where's your car, Mom?"

"Oh, I had to get an Uber here when I heard what happened."

Jade cocked her head to the side. "What? Why? What happened to your car?"

"It's a long story. Someone hit me and I didn't know if the car was safe to drive, and while I was waiting for the police to get there I got the call about you, so I just left it."

"Where did you leave your car? Where were you?"

Chief Hank turned to her. "Yeah, where were you honey?"

"Never mind that!" she said, buckling her seat belt. "What matters is that Jade is safe, and now she needs some rest. You've been through a lot."

"I'm okay," Jade said. "Chief Hank, how's Matthew? Is he okay?"

He nodded. "He's just fine. Don't worry – he's tougher than he looks."

"Good. I can't believe that he just ran in there and..." her voice cracked again, and she covered it by coughing. "It's just – if he hadn't been there – "

"No," her mom cut her off. "Don't even say it!"

"The fire is out," Chief Hank continued. "They got there pretty quickly, and half of the house is still standing. We can go back tomorrow and see what we can salvage."

"Okay," Jade said. She didn't want to think about any of that right now. All she wanted to do was crawl into a warm, fire-free bed and go to sleep. Preferably for at least twenty hours. When they got to her mom's house, that was exactly what she did.

The next morning, Jade woke up slightly disoriented. She couldn't remember why she was at her mom's house at first – then it all came flooding back.

"Oh yeah," she muttered. She slowly got herself out of bed, her head throbbing with each movement. She could hear some activity in the kitchen – a timer went off and it sounded like her mom was quite busy.

Jade smiled. She could smell something baking – no doubt her mom would have a feast ready for them. That was a nice thought, though Jade didn't feel particularly hungry.

She turned and looked at herself in the mirror, slightly horrified by what she saw. There was still some dried blood on her head, and her hair hung in greasy streaks around her face, reeking of smoke.

She quietly stepped into the bathroom and took a long shower, trying to wash the memories of the fire away.

After her shower, her head still hurt but she felt a lot better. She considered going back to bed, but the smell of coffee pulled her towards the kitchen.

She found her mom cooking up a fury and planted a kiss on her cheek. "Morning Mom."

"Good morning sweetheart." She dropped the spatula in her hand and threw her arms up for a hug. "How are you feeling?"

"Good! It was nice to clean up."

"I hope you're hungry! I've made some of your favorites – oh, and Morgan is coming by soon. I called her to let her know what happened."

"Oh, thanks. I completely forgot about that. She'd come back to the house today and just be horrified."

"Yes, so it's all taken care of! And Hank is over at the house now, trying to see what survived. You don't have to go over there today if you don't want to."

"Wow." Jade poured herself a mug of coffee. "That's really nice of him."

"He's a nice guy." The front door opened and her mom smiled. "Oh, speak of the devil! Hi honey!"

"Hello ladies!" he called out. "It's looks like we're having a fancy brunch today?"

Morgan popped her head out from behind Chief Hank. "Jade! You're alive!"

Jade laughed. "I am."

Morgan squeezed her tightly, squishing her face and swaying her from side to side. "That is the *last* time I will *ever* leave you home alone again."

Jade started laugh-coughing, which made Morgan let go.

"Oh my gosh, I'm so sorry!" Morgan said.

"It's okay." Jade took a deep breath and slowly released it. "My lungs are still a little unhappy about being filled with smoke, but they're getting better."

"Good news," Chief Hank reached into his pocket. "I found your phone in the living room. Looks like it's fine."

"Oh!" Jade accepted it from him. It looked unscathed. "Thank you so much!"

Morgan laughed. "Jade's always leaving her phone in random places – who knew it would come in handy one day. Remember that time you dropped it in the front yard and it was there all night?"

Chief Hank ignored Morgan and continued. "The bad news is that everything else looks pretty damaged."

"Ah, I kind of expected that." Jade turned her phone on and saw that she had a few missed calls – mostly from Tiffany. That was odd.

Morgan peered over her shoulder. "Why did your sister call you like ten times?"

"I don't know," Jade said with a frown. "She must've heard about the fire. I need to call her back."

"I sent everyone text messages that you were okay," her mom said, removing a tray of muffins from the oven. "But I'm sure that Tiffany and Connor will want to hear from you."

"I'll talk to them today," Jade replied.

"How about first," Morgan said, pulling Jade's wet hair back to form a braid, "you talk to *me* and explain what happened."

"There's not much to tell, really. I woke up and the house was on fire. I tried to get out but it was really smoky."

"Oh my gosh, really?"

Jade nodded. "It all happened shockingly fast. And then I fell, hit my head, and Matthew just showed up and carried me out."

"Wow," Morgan said. "I can't even be mad at him anymore if he saved your life. But...how did he beat the firefighters there?"

Chief Hank shrugged. "Someone must've called it in and he was nearby."

"I see," Morgan said. "Chief, did you have the...uh, fire people investigate it yet?"

He laughed. "Yes, the 'fire people' are on the case."

"And?" Morgan crossed her arms. "What happened?"

He rubbed his forehead. "Well, they're still trying to figure out exactly how it spread."

"What about how it *started*?" Morgan asked.

He let out a sigh. "They're pretty confident that the fire was started intentionally."

Jade and her mom both gasped.

"What?"

He took a huge bite of muffin before continuing. "Listen, before you get upset, we don't have the full story yet. But the fire started behind Morgan's window. There's evidence of an accelerant."

Jade's jaw dropped. "So you mean...someone was trying to kill me?"

"I didn't say that!" he said. "We don't have a full idea of what – "

"I knew it," her mom said. "I *knew* that someone was after you."

Jade felt like she was spinning. She had to set down her coffee mug. "I mean, there could be another explanation, right?"

"This *is* the explanation!" Morgan said. "This is crazy! We need to move!"

"Well, yes, you're going to have to move," Chief Hank said. "Because half of the house burned down."

Jade rubbed her face. "I'm so sorry Morgan. I'm so sorry that all of your stuff is gone and – "

Morgan cut her off. "Oh stop it! I don't care about any of that. I'm just glad that you're okay."

Jade smiled at her, but didn't know what to say.

"Don't worry, I've already got somewhere for you to live." Chief Hank, mouth full of muffin, cut in. "I happen to be in possession of a modest home on the west side of the island which, until recently, was undergoing renovations. I'm prepared to offer it to you for the low price of zero dollars a month."

"What!" Jade said. "That's very generous of you, but we can't live in your house without paying rent."

Morgan held up a hand. "Hang on Jade, if Chief wants to help us out, we should let him. He needs to feel useful, you know?"

Chief Hank shot her a look. "What's that supposed to mean?"

Jade's mom giggled. "Do you mean that a man of a certain age needs to feel – "

"I am not a man of a 'certain age,' " Chief said, "I just need someone to live there so the squirrels and raccoons don't take over. And I know how aggressive Morgan can be, so I thought it'd be perfect."

Morgan sighed. "I *do* hate squirrels."

"That would be really nice, until we can find somewhere else to live." Jade said before shooting Morgan a look. "And we *are* going to pay rent."

He shrugged. "You can pay the utilities if you insist. But you're really doing me a favor. I might sell it eventually, but don't have the heart to do it yet."

Morgan stuck her hand out. "You drive a tough bargain Chief, but you've got a deal."

Jade laughed. "I guess I don't have a say in this?"

"No," they both responded.

"Okay then."

Her mom shooed them into the dining room for breakfast. Jade did as she was told, quietly amused by Morgan continuing to bargain with Chief Hank about what was included with their new rental. Morgan seemed to think that access to the boat went along with the house, which Chief Hank was vehemently denying.

Jade didn't have much to add – she was too overwhelmed to joke around. The thought of moving, contacting her insurance, getting a new computer for work...it seemed like so much.

But, at the same time, it was easier to focus on those tasks than the possibility that someone was trying to kill her.

Chapter 13

After the breakfast feast, Morgan volunteered to go back to the house with Chief to see if anything in her room was salvageable. She also promised Jade that she'd handle telling their landlord the bad news.

"I hope you girls had rental insurance," Chief said as they got into his car.

"Don't worry, we did. I'm guessing that it'll be weeks before we can get things replaced, though."

He sighed. "Yeah, it's not going to be an easy process. But you're welcome to everything in my house."

"Thanks Chief. I actually had a lot of my stuff with me because Luke and I were doing a shoot off of the island. Plus, I don't really have a lot of stuff."

Chief laughed. "Nothing that can't fit in your backpack, right?"

She thought for a moment. "Right. Well actually, I was starting to get too much extra junk and it was getting cluttered. So now I can start over fresh and make sure that I'm not buying things that I don't need."

"Or you could get a bigger backpack?"

"Sure."

Morgan was happy to joke around for a distraction – anything to get her mind off of the fact that someone started that fire on purpose.

"So Chief," she said, trying to keep her tone casual. "What are the chances that we catch whoever did this?"

"I don't know." He frowned. "So far it doesn't look like anything was left behind. But we're going to question people and look for witnesses. Someone had to see something."

Morgan let out a sigh. "You know how *that* goes..."

"Oh I know. Matthew is already out today questioning people. I can check in with him to see how it's going."

"I'm sure that Luke would be happy to offer his services again if we need anyone to confess."

Chief chuckled. "I'll keep that in mind."

Morgan smiled to herself. Luke was extremely worried about her, going so far as to suggest that he'd force his room-mates to share a room so she and Jade could move into their house. He also insisted that Matthew would then *have to* share his gun with him, and that Luke planned to get a Wild West style holster for it.

Unfortunately, none of that was realistic.

They got to the house and Morgan stood for a moment, in awe of how the fire ate away at their home. For some reason, she'd imagined that Jade's room would be damaged but everything else would look the same.

That wasn't the case. They carefully navigated getting inside and Morgan was shocked to see that almost everything in her room was damaged. The walls were blackened and there was soot and ash on everything. She peeked into a few areas only to find that everything she was looking for was destroyed.

Chief quietly watched from what used to be the doorway.

Finally, she stood up and dusted off her hands. "I don't know what I expected it to look like...but I didn't expect this."

He put a hand on her shoulder. "Sorry kid. I'm glad you weren't here."

"Me too. I don't think that Matthew could've carried both of us at the same time."

He laughed and they went back outside. He asked her to wait by the car so he could check in with the deputy who was working in the area where the fire started.

Morgan decided to take the opportunity to give their landlord a call. She was dreading it, but she needed to get it over with.

To her surprise, he was already aware of the fire – the sheriff's office called to tell him. He also knew that they were okay, because his daughter still lived on the island and the fire was the talk of the town.

A car pulled into the driveway and Morgan watched as a well dressed woman got out of the driver's seat. Was the insurance adjuster here already?

She ended her conversation with the landlord and started walking toward the woman.

"Can I help you?" Morgan asked.

She jumped and turned around. "Oh! Hey!"

"Oh, Tiffany! I didn't recognize you. What're you doing here?"

She took off her sunglasses and stared at the house for a moment. "I wanted to surprise everyone with a visit. I got this weird text from mom saying not to worry about the fire, and that you and Jade were okay?"

Morgan laughed. "And that was all that it said?"

"Yeah. I had no idea that your *house* burned down!"

"Oh this?" Morgan swooped a hand across the scene. "This is the hot new way to get an open floor plan."

"What happened? Were you guys home?"

Morgan shook her head. "Jade was home. But she got out, thankfully."

Tiffany nodded but said nothing. Morgan tore her eyes away from the house to look at her – all of the color had disappeared from Tiffany's face. "Are you okay?"

"Oh – yes. I just...can't believe this."

Morgan rubbed her forehead. "It gets worse. They think someone started the fire."

"What do you mean?"

"Like, on purpose."

Tiffany slightly stumbled back onto her car. "I think I need to sit down."

Oy, she *really* didn't look good. "Yeah, of course. Why don't you take a seat?"

Tiffany nodded and pulled at the car door, but it was locked.

Morgan had an idea. "Jade is at your mom's house. How about we go over there – I'll drive. I rode here with Chief, and he's talking to some fire investigators, or whatever they are. I'll let him know that you're here and then we can go?"

"That sounds good."

Morgan went around the back of the house to tell Chief that she was leaving. The scorched look of the backyard caught her off guard. It was unbelievable that Jade was able to get out.

Well, she didn't really get out. Matthew carried her out. And actually, he was kind of an idiot for running into a burning house like that.

But the good kind of idiot.

"Hey Chief – Tiffany just stopped by."

He turned to look at her. "Wait – who?"

Morgan sighed. "You know, your *other* step-daughter. You only have two. Try to keep up."

"Sorry," he said with a laugh. "I didn't know she was coming to visit."

"Anyway, I'm going to catch a ride with her back to Margie's house."

"You mean back to *my* house?" He said, lifting his eyebrows.

"Alright." Morgan smiled. "I guess that *is* your house now. And your old house is now *my* house."

"Squatter," he muttered before turning back to work.

She laughed – a real belly laugh. It was nice having someone like Chief on their side.

Morgan spent the entire drive telling Tiffany about the fire and all the issues and threats surrounding the Colby Farm project.

"So basically, now we'll have to convince Jade to stop with all this nonsense before she gets herself killed."

Tiffany shot her a look. "What? She can't stop now. She can't let them win."

"Are you crazy? They *actually* tried to kill her!"

Tiffany shook her head. "No, they just started a fire."

"How are you not seeing how that's the same as trying to kill her!"

"Well, first of all, it didn't seem like the person who left that message on the barn was some kind of mastermind," Tiffany said. "They didn't even spell 'hurt' correctly. And if they wanted to kill her, there are easier ways to do that without attracting so much attention."

"I can't even talk to you right now, because you've clearly lost your mind."

Tiffany laughed. "I don't know, it seems like they were just...trying to send a message. Everything they've done so far sounds like it was a warning. And there'll be no stopping Jade now. You'll see."

Morgan groaned. There was no way that this entire family could be *that* crazy.

They walked into Margie's and once everyone got over the excitement of Tiffany being there, Morgan decided to take a stand and tell Jade that she had to stop anything having to do with the Colby Farm vote.

"I'm not going to stop," Jade said calmly. "And I'm not going to be scared by this."

Okay, so that was *two* Cliftons who were out of their minds.

Surely Margie wouldn't allow it? Morgan shot her a pleading look.

Margie cleared her throat. "Honey, don't you think that you've done enough? Is it really worth it?"

"Of course it is. Look how hard they're trying to fight me. It means they're afraid that I'll win."

"Can I counter," said Morgan, "that they seem to be willing to *kill* for this? So how will you compete with that?"

Jade flinched. "The police will catch them. Chief Hank will figure out who it was."

Morgan threw her hands up, exasperated. "*Hello*! Do you remember how long it took them to catch my mom's killer?"

Jade nodded. "Yes. But the vote is only four weeks away, so I just have to survive that long."

Margie put her hands on her hips. "And then after four weeks you don't care if you survive?"

Jade laughed, reaching out to grab her mom's hand. "No, Mom. Of course I care. But after that, I'll have already won."

"Jade's right," Tiffany added. "She can't give in now."

"I feel like you've both lost your minds," Morgan continued, "and we need to separate you before you come up with any more bad ideas."

Tiffany shifted uncomfortably. "Oh that's too bad, because I don't have anywhere to stay."

"You can stay with me!" Margie said.

Tiffany made a face. "No, I can't stay with newlyweds. Sorry Mom, but you guys are kissy all of the time."

"I mean..." Morgan tried not to crack a smile. "She's right."

"You can stay with us," Jade said. "Chief Hank is letting us move into his old house. How long is your visit?"

Tiffany shrugged her shoulders. "I haven't decided yet."

What? Were they living in the twilight zone right now?

The house burns down and Tiffany just shows up and encourages Jade to be reckless? And doesn't know how long she'll be here? Did *her* house burn down, too?

That was an odd way to frame a visit, but neither Jade nor Margie questioned it. They were just excited that Tiffany was there.

Morgan didn't know what her game was, but she'd find out eventually. In the meantime, she had to keep Jade alive. It seemed that it was going to be no easy task to keep her beautiful, stubborn goat of a friend out of trouble.

Morgan let out a sigh. This was going to be a long four weeks.

Chapter 14

As excited as Jade was about seeing Tiffany, it didn't feel like they had time to catch up – there was *so much* that they needed to do at Chief Hank's place. For the past few months, he'd been slowly working on improvement projects – both on his own and with various contractors. The projects were mostly done, but nothing was cleaned up, and the house wasn't exactly livable yet.

On top of that, Jade felt anxious that their insurance policy might require them to file a claim within twenty four hours or something. She'd lost everything in the fire, though, so she had no way of even *finding* their policy. Luckily Morgan still had her computer and promised to take care of it.

"I'll figure it out and then we can send them a list of all the stuff that we lost."

Jade frowned. "Do you think it'll be that easy?"

"I don't know," Morgan said with a shrug. "It doesn't matter though. We'll figure it out. Don't worry."

Jade had to force herself to smile. She still felt awful. It felt like the fire was her fault – maybe she *did* accidentally cause the fire to start somehow? This idea that someone started the fire was...terrifying. She'd much prefer if it was just a freak accident, even if it was her own fault.

In fact, there was a good chance that it *was* an accident. She decided to wait for the final report from the specialists before she would worry.

Being able to put that out of her mind was helpful in planning the rest of the day. Her goal was to get Chief Hank's house to the point that they'd be able to spend the night there. She didn't want to impose on her hosts' hospitality too long – though her mom seemed *thrilled* to have them visiting, maybe Chief Hank didn't feel the same?

Jade just remembered how angry Brandon would get if she had anyone stay longer than a night – he'd never say anything to the guests but would stomp around the house until they left. It made everything tense.

Not that Chief Hank was like Brandon but...it still worried her. The last thing she wanted was to be a bother, and it felt like that was all she'd been to anyone recently.

After telling her mom her plan to move to her "new place" as soon as possible, they argued for about half an hour until Jade agreed to spend at least one more night at her mom's.

"Can't you give your old mom *one* night?" she insisted. "It'll be fun!"

"I know it'll be fun Mom, but we really need to..."

"Oh hush!" She stopped and pointed a finger at Jade. "And one more thing. You are *not* moving into that house until there are cameras installed and running. I don't care how long it takes and I don't want to hear any complaints!"

Jade put her hands up. "Okay, okay! I won't fight you this time."

The first step was going to the house to assess what needed to be done and to make a list of things that they wanted to buy. There wasn't much – Chief Hank had the basics.

Morgan wanted some blackout curtains for her room and a new duvet set for the bed. Jade decided that it might be nice to get her own bed set as well, just to make it feel a little more like home. Even Tiffany decided to get in on the fun and buy some decorations.

After that, they spent a few hours shopping before returning to face the task of cleaning Chief Hank's house. There was random stuff everywhere – discarded tools, stiff paint brushes that were never cleaned, even piles of wood dust from sawing.

Morgan put some music on and they got to work. Jade was surprised by how much fun they were having. At one point, she laughed until she started crying.

It was a great day, really – as long as she could keep the fire out of her mind. Most of the time it wasn't too hard, because it wasn't something that she wanted to think about. But occasionally, a flashback and a feeling of panic would break into her mind and stop her in her tracks.

They got pretty close to finishing cleaning, but her mom insisted that they go back to her house for dinner and a night of board games. Luke stopped by, apologizing that he hadn't come sooner – there were a few time-dependent issues that he needed to handle for the photography business.

"Can you believe that I trust this guy with that kind of stuff?" Morgan said in a hushed voice.

Tiffany nodded her head. "I can. He's beautiful."

"Tiffany!" Jade said. "You can't – "

It was no use, though. Morgan was already laughing, and Tiffany joined in.

"He really is a *beautiful* man," Morgan said with a sigh. "And shockingly, he's also really smart. And nice. And funny."

"Ugh," Tiffany put up a hand. "I get it. Despite your house burning down, you're still the luckiest girl on the island."

Morgan beamed. "I am."

"So," Tiffany cleared her throat and raised her voice. "When do I get to meet the heroic Matthew?"

Jade felt her body tense. She'd meant to call Matthew and thank him for what he'd done, but that seemed lame. She felt that it should be something that she did in person, but she'd been so busy that day that it was easy to come up with excuses why it wasn't the right time.

Truth be told, she was nervous to see him again. Plus, she didn't want to take away time from his weekend...especially if he was busy with Laura.

Luke swooped in and gave Morgan a kiss on the cheek. "Ah, I did try to convince him to come over, but the man is on a rampage."

"Is he?" Morgan asked.

Luke nodded. "Oh yes. He's been interrogating people all day. I couldn't even get him to take a break for dinner when I ran into him in town. I had to throw a burrito at him from afar."

"Oh, that sounds like him," Morgan nodded. "Typical heroic Matthew stuff."

Jade smiled but pretended like she was very focused on her playing cards. It was probably better that Matthew wasn't coming – it would be hard to thank him with everyone else around. They'd already come up with a nickname for him, and there was a chance that her awkward but sincere thanks could turn into a big joke. And she wouldn't want that, because what he'd done for her wasn't a joke.

On Sunday, Morgan volunteered to finish preparing their insurance claim while Jade went over to Chief Hank's house to get a head start on the rest of the cleaning. She'd made a discovery late the night before that there were some things left behind in the fridge that had grown unbelievably moldy. On top of that, there were spills and sticky spots that needed a lot of attention.

She was scrubbing a particularly stubborn mystery spot when her mom called.

"Hey honey! I'm running to the store. Do you want me to get you something, like some soda...or pepper spray?"

Jade laughed. "I don't think I need pepper spray, no. Maybe a baseball bat? Or a dog."

"I can help with that," chimed a voice from the front door.

Jade jumped at the sound, dropping her phone.

Thankfully, it was just Matthew. Though as soon as she saw him, her nerves flared and she wondered if maybe she'd prefer to face an intruder – or the arsonist.

"Oh – I'm sorry! I didn't mean to scare you," he said. "The door was open."

"It's okay, I was just in my own little world!" Jade stooped to pick up her phone. "Sorry Mom, I dropped you. Matthew just stopped by, is it okay if I call you back?"

"Yes," she said, "tell him I can't wait to see him again – and I have to find some way to thank him and I was thinking – "

"Okay Mom," Jade said, "I'll talk to you later. Love you!"

"Love you too!"

She set her phone down and tried to smile as naturally as possible. "Sorry about that. My mom is still pretty freaked out about the fire."

"That's why I'm here!" He set a large bag on the table. "To install your new surveillance system."

Jade laughed. "I'm sorry that you got dragged into this – I think you've already done more than enough."

"Oh, I'm happy to help."

Jade took a step forward. It didn't matter how uneasy her insides felt – she finally had her chance to talk to him and she needed to take it. "I wasn't able to properly thank you for what you did. I don't even know the words. You saved my life."

He shook his head and smiled that dazzling smile. "Really, I was just doing my job. I'm glad I was there."

"Me too," Jade said. "And really – thank you."

They both smiled, but said nothing. Jade tried to reach into the bag at the same time as Matthew reached to open it, and their hands met. She quickly pulled away and retreated to the fridge.

"I just need to finish up a few shelves here and then I can help you," she said.

She was grateful to be able to turn away from him. She thought that her face might be a bit red. Even getting that thank you out was tough – and it didn't feel like it was nearly enough to convey how grateful she was, but she didn't know what else to say.

And then – he brushed it off so coolly. How many burning buildings had he run into by this point in his career? It was so like him to refuse any praise.

But it *was* true that he was just doing his job – she shouldn't read into it. No matter how dizzy she felt when she saw him, or how stunning he looked in that uniform, she had to remind herself – he was just doing his job.

"I see that Chief treats the refrigerator the same way here as he does at the office," Matthew called out from the other side of the kitchen.

"Yeah," Jade rubbed her forehead. "I've been working on it for a while."

"Well, don't let me interfere," he said. "I'll get to work."

Jade didn't want him to leave now that they'd broken the ice. "Have you, uh, set up cameras before?"

"Not exactly, and I don't want to jinx myself, but I *think* I can finagle it."

Jade slapped herself in the forehead. "Oh *duh*, you're an engineer. Of course you know how to set up a few cameras."

He smiled but said nothing; instead, he stepped outside and returned a moment later with a ladder.

Jade silently berated herself to stop being awkward and get back to work. Luckily, Matthew spent the rest of his time busily drilling and hammering away, so Jade didn't have a chance to say any other stupid things.

She only finished with the fridge when he was just about finished. As he was packing up, he showed her the instructions for the cameras.

"You can watch the live video from your phone or laptop."

Jade frowned. "My phone is the only thing that actually survived the fire."

"Oh." His face fell. "That's terrible – I'm sorry."

She shook her head. "No, no – I don't mean to complain. I just mean that the phone will have to do for now. You know, to complete this security suite."

He laughed. "I got you. Actually, you know what – I have a laptop at home that I don't use very often. It was my old work laptop, but when I quit, I got to take it with me. Let me run home and – "

"No, please, you've already done so much."

He shrugged. "No, really – I'd be happy if it'd make this transition a little easier."

Jade thought she'd melt into a puddle. "Well – if you insist."

He flashed a smile before disappearing to his car.

She didn't know what had gotten into her – she was almost being a little *flirty*. It must've been the smoke inhalation. She tried to pull herself together, but as soon as he was back, she felt herself getting loopy again.

"Here you go – one mid tier laptop for your security super system," he said, handing her the laptop.

"Thanks again – you've seriously just done too much."

"I'm glad I could help. Well, I'd better get back to work and find out who started that fire."

"So...you really think someone did it on purpose?"

He frowned. "Unfortunately, yes. I don't have any suspects yet – but I've got a good feeling that we'll crack it."

"When is your next day off? I'd like to repay you – some-how – even in a little way."

He smiled. Man – was his smile always that bright white? Or did the fire do something to it?

"That's very kind of you, but I'm not taking any time off until I figure out what happened."

Of course.

How could she ever have doubted how great of a guy he was? And how could she ever have thought that he was inter-ested in *her*...

"Well, you have to take a break eventually. I have to do *something* to thank you – I can make you dinner? Or – dessert or something?"

Obviously he wouldn't want to have a *dinner* with her. She didn't mean for it to sound like she was suggesting some romantic date – it just came out weird.

He crossed his arms. "Actually, you could do me a favor."

Don't stare at his muscles. Don't stare at his muscles. "Anything. Anything you need."

"I'd feel a lot better if you let me add one more security feature."

She tilted her head. "Okay?"

"Well, I know you mentioned that you wanted a dog – you know, for some extra protection. And Toast is going to be pretty lonely since I haven't been home much recently. Maybe I could drop him off before my shift and you guys can keep each other company? He's a pretty good guard dog, and I'm fairly certain that he'd eat any intruders without question."

Jade laughed. "That sounds really nice, actually. I think we'd make quite a pair."

"I think so too. Okay – well, I'll bring him by tomorrow morning then?"

"Sure! I'll be here. I'll probably still be cleaning the fridge."

He laughed. "Sounds good. Stay safe Jade."

"You too!"

You too?

So much for not saying dumb things. Oh well. She'd tried but...it seemed there were two things she could no longer deny.

The first was that if level-headed Matthew thought that someone set her house on fire, then someone *really did* set her house on fire. And the second was that she was hopelessly, maddeningly powerless over her feelings for him.

Jade couldn't decide which of these two truths was worse.

Chapter 15

Toast got his first assignment at Jade's place on Monday morning. Matthew chuckled to himself as he watched Toast leap into the car, panting excitedly – Toast didn't get to go a lot of places, so he was thrilled despite not knowing *where* he was going.

Generally car rides meant good things for him – oceanside walks, ice cream, and getting to explore Luke's house. That was normally fun – despite the over abundance of people who wanted to pet him when he got there.

Matthew parked his car outside of Chief Hank's – er, Jade's house – and Toast whined until he was allowed to leap out onto the lawn. His tail was up and wagging, and he was eagerly sniffing everything in his path.

At least he seemed to be in a good mood. Matthew walked up to the front door and called Jade's phone – he didn't want to wake anyone else up by knocking if they were still sleeping.

Jade opened the door after three rings. "Good morning!"

"Morning!"

Toast stood, frozen, staring at her.

Jade lowered herself to the ground and pulled something out from behind her back. "Hi Toast, I've been waiting for you!"

His ears perked up when he heard her voice, and when he saw the large treat in her hand, his tail started wagging manically.

"I'm sorry – is it okay if I give this to him? I picked up a few things at the store."

Matthew smiled. "Of course. He loves food. And he's still pretty skinny, so he can use some extra treats."

Jade smiled and moved her hand closer to Toast. "Go ahead...good boy!"

Toast didn't hesitate, pouncing on the treat before proudly trotting around as if he were showing it off. After a moment, he flopped down on the ground and got to work on eating.

"Wow – I'm glad that he seems to remember you," Matthew commented. "He's not scared at all."

"There's nothing to be scared of," Jade said with a smile. "We have high tech, twenty four hour surveillance here."

Matthew laughed. "That's right. Are the cameras working well?"

"They are, thank you again. My mom keeps asking if she can login to watch the video feed, but I'm afraid to give her the password. I think she'll just sit at home all day, watching, and probably never sleep again."

"The first steps into madness," he said, before hurriedly adding, "Not that I think your mom is crazy or anything."

Jade smiled. "I think she's just crazy worried. But she doesn't need to be, because we've got you on the case! I know you'll figure out who's been trying to terrorize us."

He couldn't take one more nice compliment from her, so he changed the subject. "Of course. Well, good luck with him. If he's annoying or tries to bite someone, just give me a call and I'll come back and get him."

"Oh he would *never* bite anyone!" Jade said, patting Toast on the head.

Toast looked up at her, opened his mouth, and then closed his eyes; he looked like he was in bliss.

"Are there any rules that I should know?" she asked.

Matthew shrugged. "Not really. I brought his dog food so you can feed him if you like. He usually eats at seven. I might be done by then but...I'm not sure. Also, he's not allowed to jump on people. And he's not allowed to steal things, obviously, so keep an eye on your toaster."

"He'll be good. Don't worry. We'll go for some nice long walks and maybe even a drive later."

"You hear that Toast? This is going to be better than doggy daycare."

"It is!" Jade said. "Well – thanks. Have a nice day."

"You too."

When Matthew got back to his car, he looked back one last time to see that the front door was closed and that Jade was safely inside. It felt like the weight on his chest was lessening, even by just a bit.

Toast really took to Jade, and Matthew knew that he'd bark at any little sound that he heard. Maybe that would be enough to spook anyone lurking around the house. And if they were foolish enough to try to break in again – well, Toast could take care of that, too.

Matthew decided to wait outside of the house for a few minutes just in case Toast was misbehaving and needed to go back home. For a moment, he closed his eyes – it felt nice to let them rest. He hadn't gotten much sleep over the weekend, because the idea of the suspect getting away drove him mad.

He couldn't stop until he figured out what happened. Every time that he closed his eyes, he could see Jade's face as clear as day – the blood on the side of her forehead, her beautiful green eyes reddened from the smoke. He remembered how her weight felt as he carried her, and how she wrapped her arms around his neck...

Dispatch came over the radio, snapping him out of his daydream. Actually, it seemed like he was almost dozing off. Maybe he'd try to get a little more sleep tonight.

He sighed and started the car. It was time to get back to work.

Over the weekend, he managed to track down and interview sixteen different groups of people who attended Jade's fundraiser. In total, he talked to nearly forty people, and still, no one had seen anything suspicious at the barn. People had their theories of who was to blame, of course, but no one had any evidence.

He'd already visited all of Jade's old neighbors to see if anyone had video footage that might point him in the direction of a suspect. Unfortunately, no one had anything useful. One neighbor had a doorbell camera, but the scope of the video didn't show anything for the entire night until the fire started. Whoever started the fire must've stayed in the backyard, and it was too dark to see anything back there even if they had a camera.

He decided that the first person he'd talk to today would be Barb. Unlike the last time they spoke, she was more than willing to talk to him.

"I'm *horrified* about what happened to that girl!" she said. "I mean, I disagreed with her, but this is just too far!"

"I agree. So do you have any idea who might've done it?"

Barb shook her head vigorously. "No. But if I hear *anything* I will tell you straight away. I don't want to be involved with this project anymore. I'm completely removing myself from it and going neutral. I'm advising that other business owners on the island do the same."

"Oh? Is anyone fighting you on this?"

She frowned. "Not really. Though when I told the county council, they said it was a shame."

"Who said it was a shame?"

"Jared. You know him, the kid in the suit."

Matthew smiled. Jared wasn't really a kid – he must've been at least thirty. But Barb thought that everyone under the age of sixty was a kid. "Yeah, I think I know him."

"I mean, he wasn't fighting me on it. He said it was a shame because it's important for the county to have a healthy discussion."

"I see."

What were the chances that someone else from the San Juan Small Business Association disagreed with Barb's decision to withdraw her support for the sale of Colby's land? Hopefully they wouldn't take any action against her, too; but it wasn't like she was coming out in favor of Jade's plan. She was only declaring herself neutral, like Switzerland. Swiss Barb. From now on that's how Matthew would think of her.

She put her hands up. "I don't want to be a part of *any* kind of discussion where people are violent! And starting fires! I mean – that's just unbelievable. Just *unbelievable*! Nothing is worth that. I'm going to mind my own business from now on."

"Alright Barb, it was nice talking to you. If anything comes up, call."

"I will."

Barb's alibi checked out – she'd hosted a party at her home on the night of the fire. He decided that it might be a good idea to talk to the county council and see if they had heard any complaints about Barb's withdrawal from the vote. He was about to call for the phone numbers of the members when his phone rang.

"Hello?"

"Hey babe, it's me."

He cringed. He'd forgotten to call Laura back last night like he said he would. "Hey – what's up?"

"You tell me. I haven't heard from you all day."

"I know – I'm sorry. I'm really involved in trying to figure out this case and I forgot to call last night. I just fell asleep when I got home."

Laura sighed. "I mean I get that this is important, but you already saved the day. Can't someone else work on this? Don't you, like, get a break or something now?"

Matthew laughed. "Well – everyone's pretty busy, and I'm not the only one working on this. I really want to help with it."

She was quiet for a moment. "Okay."

"I'll call you tonight, okay?"

"I guess."

"Hey – don't be mad. I'll make it up to you."

"Alright. Well – good luck today."

"Thanks."

He didn't know the next time that he'd be able to see her, and she was already not happy with him. If only he could combine seeing her with work somehow...

Oh yeah! Burke Development was throwing another party on Lopez island. Matthew couldn't miss it. Maybe Laura could be a useful second set of eyes? She'd like that – to be involved. It was hard for her to feel left out. Plus she'd love getting dressed up and going to a fancy party. That was the part Matthew was *less* interested in.

Perfect – there was the solution. He set a reminder on his phone to call her; hopefully she'd be excited by the idea.

Chapter 16

Jade's stomach leapt when she saw that Matthew was calling.

"Hey!"

"Hey, what's up?"

"Oh nothing really, how about you?"

"I wanted to let you know that I'm planning on coming to the party to scope things out, and Laura wanted to help too."

"That'll be great!" Jade heard herself speak the words out loud, adding *just* enough inflection to make them sound true.

"Great! I'll see there?"

"Yeah, see you then."

Jade hung up the phone and buried her face in her hands. She had suspected that the conversation would likely be related to her house burning down, and not to like...to ask her out or to chat. But she hadn't expected the Laura curveball. She let out a groan – what a mess.

"What's wrong?" Tiffany said, popping her head through the doorway.

"Oh – nothing. Just getting ready to go to that party on Lopez Island."

"Ah, the one thrown by your competition?"

She nodded. "Do you think it's a bad idea? Do you think I'm...I don't know, provoking the enemy?"

Tiffany took a seat next to her on the bed. "I know mom's worried about that, but I don't think so. I think that showing up at the party shows you won't be bullied."

"Really?"

"Yeah! You have to go. And who knows? Maybe the person who's after you will do something really stupid and expose themselves."

Jade laughed. "That'd be great. Because Matthew interviewed a ton of people and he's still no closer to figuring out who did it."

"Is he going to this thing too?"

"Yeah, and Laura."

Tiffany tilted her head. "Who's Laura again?"

"His girlfriend."

She made a face. "Oh. So you're stuck being the third wheel?"

"I guess," Jade shrugged. "Morgan and Luke would come but they're busy with a wedding."

Tiffany's eyes brightened. "I'll be your date!"

"Really? Are you sure that you're not busy?"

"No! I think it'll be fun. We can get dressed up!"

Jade wasn't sure why her sister had so much free time all of a sudden, but she wasn't going to question it. Not that Tiffany would tell her anyway.

"Okay! I don't really have anything nice to wear but...I'll give it my best shot!"

"What time do we need to leave?"

"I'd say we have about an hour before we need to catch the ferry."

"Alright, then I need to get ready *now*."

Jade laughed. "Oh, okay. How dressed up are you going to be?"

Tiffany flashed a smile but said nothing; she just ran off to her room without another word.

It would be good to have Tiffany on her side. She had a lot of experience with business and she'd already volunteered to join Jade's makeshift committee. She was happy for the help, but she wasn't sure how long her sister planned to stay on the island. Would she still be around when the vote happened?

Every time she asked her about it, Tiffany would brush it off. Once she gave the excuse that her vacation time was close to maxing out so she needed to take a few weeks. But then when Morgan asked her about it, she said she was on a sabbatical.

It was very unlike Tiffany to take time off – the most she ever took was a week to visit their mom, or a few days around Christmas. Though she always talked about how one day she'd like to visit Paris and London, she never had time. Work was too busy and too important to her. So why would she waste her free time on Jade's silly little project?

Jade knew better than to keep asking questions, though. When – actually, *if* – Tiffany decided to tell her what was going on, it would be on her own terms. They were much closer now than when they were growing up, but Tiffany was still very much an older sister. She liked to keep her secrets.

About ten minutes before they needed to leave, Tiffany came back into Jade's room.

"What do you think?" she asked, spinning around in a gorgeous green and gold dress.

"You look great." Jade sighed, looking down at the skirt she'd chosen. She felt positively frumpy next to Tiffany – she just didn't have as nice of a wardrobe. Or as much confidence. "This is the best I could come up with."

"You look nice!" Tiffany said. "But if you don't like your outfit, do you want to borrow something?"

Jade shook her head. "Oh – I don't think that anything you have would fit."

"What, you think it'd all be too big?"

Jade laughed. It was nice of her sister to pretend that she couldn't see the extra jiggle in her step. "No – the opposite. It'd definitely be too small."

Tiffany rolled her eyes. "Oh stop. I have the perfect dress for you. Hang on a second."

She ran out of the room and returned with a form-fitting red dress. "I have this little golden belt too, which I think will be the perfect touch."

Jade bit her lip. "I don't know..."

"Just try it on! You don't have to wear it."

Jade accepted the dress and decided to give it a shot. She was surprised that it fit – it was definitely a bit more snug on her than it would be on Tiffany, but it didn't look ridiculous or anything. And the belt was a nice touch – it made her look sharp. Professional, even.

"Okay, you can come back," Jade called out once she had a moment to look at herself.

Tiffany opened the door and let out a little squeal. "You look awesome! Do you like it?"

"I think so. Do you think it's okay?"

Tiffany nodded. "Definitely. You look great. That dress is made for you – you should keep it."

"Tiffany! I'm not going to steal your clothes."

She shrugged. "It's not stealing if I give it to you. And I have so many dresses that I won't need anymore."

"What do you mean?"

"Oh," Tiffany took a look at her watch. "We have to go, right?"

Jade startled when she saw how late it was. "Oh shoot – we do. C'mon!"

Luckily, the ferry was late and they were able to catch it without any issue. The trip was short and the entire time, Tiffany was cracking her up with stories about her coworkers.

They got off of the ferry on Lopez Island and were soon driving up Ferry Road, the lush green forest parting for the steady flow of cars. It was one of the things that Jade loved so much about the islands – even in the winter time, they were vibrant and brimming with life. Not as much as in the summer, of course, but it was always beautiful and green.

They got to the events center and quickly found a parking spot.

"Morgan told me that this building was actually built by a friend of Eric Burke."

Tiffany stood back, taking in the sight. "That's the guy who owns the company?"

Jade nodded. "Yeah – well, he didn't start the company, his dad did. But he's running this project, I guess."

"This building is a monstrosity," Tiffany said. "If they make something like this on San Juan, it'll stick out like a sore thumb."

"I agree, but it's not really up to me. Are you ready to go in?"

"Yes! Let's go."

Once again, there were waiters circulating the room, carry-ing trays of champagne and appetizers. But this time, they'd stepped up their game. Beautiful flowers covered almost every surface; there were even arrangements hanging on the walls. In the center of the room, an enormous ice sculpture spouted a neon blue drink that guests captured in drinking glasses.

Everything just looked *nice* – and expensive. To top it all off, there seemed to be twice as many people at this event than at the last one.

"Oh look – there's another room. Want to take a peek?" asked Tiffany.

Jade sighed. "I guess. You'd think that this room wasn't fancy enough."

Tiffany shrugged. "I'm not impressed."

As they got closer to the next room, the music grew louder and their eardrums were assaulted by heavy bass. People were dancing and shouting over the music. There was a DJ booth in the corner – Jade squinted at it, and then was overcome with horror.

"We need to get out of here."

"What? Why?" Tiffany asked.

Jade tried to force Tiffany to turn around and leave, but it was too late. He'd spotted them.

"Jade! Hey, Jade!"

She cringed. There was no running now.

"Hey Brandon, how are you?"

"I'm great! They booked me for this, isn't this party awesome?"

Tiffany shrugged. "Not really."

Brandon's smile faded. "Wait, are you okay Jade? I saw the news about the fire – "

"I'm fine," she said. "No harm done."

Brandon shook his head. "I'm really sorry that happened to you and I'm glad that you're okay."

Jade smiled and thanked him; she felt bad that she'd tried to avoid him. But in her defense, she never knew which Brandon she would get – but today it seemed she'd gotten happy Brandon. Happy that he'd booked this gig, and even a bit sweet about the fire.

"You'd better get back to work," Tiffany said, shooing him away. "You don't want to get sacked."

Brandon laughed. "That's right! Well – it was nice seeing you!

"You too."

And just like that, he walked off.

"That could've been much worse," said Jade.

"You're right," Tiffany said. "I was imagining trying to get him fired as payback for how he treated you during the divorce."

Jade laughed. "That's all in the past."

Tiffany raised an eyebrow. "Oh don't act like you don't hold grudges."

"I don't." She paused for a moment, shifting her weight. The shoes she'd chosen to go with this dress weren't the most comfortable. Maybe she should've stuck with the frumpy outfit. "Do you want to go back to the other room? This is so loud and I don't recognize anyone."

Tiffany nodded. "Okay."

They wandered back into the main room, stopping to look at some of the different "propaganda points," as Tiffany called them. There was a new promotional video – better than the last one, but still missing the mark. It showed a few shots of bald eagles but then cut to a woman in a large hat sitting under an umbrella. It seemed like they were still advertising for the wrong kind of island.

Jade kept looking around, trying to see if anyone was watching her. It didn't feel like it, but she felt a little paranoid.

A few people stopped to talk to them and give their condolences about the fire.

Apparently, it had been all over the local news. She didn't know how to respond to people – saying thank you seemed strange. Like what was she thanking them for? But what else was she supposed to say? The whole thing was just awkward.

They'd been there for almost an hour and Jade was starting to get restless. She thought about texting Matthew, but decided against it. What if he was caught up in work? Tiffany suggested that he was at the party, but working undercover.

The thought of it made Jade laugh. "I think it'd be hard for him to blend in. He's really tall."

"Is that right?" Tiffany said. "Is he cute, too?"

"Decide for yourself," Jade said with a smile, motioning towards the door. Matthew had just walked in.

Tiffany turned around. "Oh. *Oh*! And that's the girlfriend?"

Jade nodded.

"What's she like?"

"I don't really know. I've only met her a handful of times. But she seems nice."

Jade was about to wave them over when someone stepped into her line of sight – Eric Burke.

"Jane, how nice to see you!"

She considered correcting him but didn't know how without sounding like a jerk. "Hi Eric, nice to see you too. You've thrown another lovely party."

He made a slight bow. "Thank you, thank you. I had some help this time."

Jade motioned to her right. "This is my sister Tiffany. Tiffany, this is Eric. He's the one in charge of – well, all of this."

Tiffany flashed a brief smile. "It's nice to meet you."

"Hang on a second." Eric clapped his hands together. "You know, my operation's a family affair too."

Eric raised his arms, trying to wave someone to come over. Jade turned to see where he was motioning. Across the room was a sharply dressed man in a grey suit. He saw Eric and seemed to ignore him at first, but the waving grew wild and he had no choice but to come over.

"Ah, there he is! Sidney, this is Tiffany and Jane. And ladies, this is my cousin Sidney."

Sidney nodded, the dark features of his face remaining unchanged. "How do you do?"

"This is the woman I was telling you about – the activist! My competition!"

Sidney focused his eyes on Jade. She had to remind herself not to shrink down – despite how uncomfortable his gaze made her. He had intense, dark brown eyes and he lacked the good humor of his cousin. "It was nice of you to come. Please excuse me."

He walked off, and Eric laughed. "Sorry about him, he's always been really serious. Even when we were kids."

"Do you find it difficult working with family?" asked Tiffany.

"Oh, no I wouldn't say that. He's extremely focused, which is great. I mean, I'm focused on getting this project done too. Only a few weeks until the vote!"

Jade cleared her throat. "Yeah, two weeks."

"Two? Oh, I must've lost track of the time. To be honest, Sidney is more of the details person. I'm the guy with the big ideas."

Jade smiled. Even if he couldn't get her name right, his excitement was contagious – almost child like. His lack of attention to detail might explain the tropical themed videos, too...

"I don't mean to interrupt, but I wanted to say hello." Matthew cautiously stepped into their circle.

"Hello!" Eric clapped a hand on his shoulder. "You're not interrupting, we're just catching up."

Laura smiled and extended a hand. "Hi, it's nice to meet you. I'm Matthew's girlfriend Laura."

"Great to meet you – oh, that's right! I saw Matthew on the news. Amazing work with that fire – and wow, I'm really forgetting myself. So sorry to hear about what happened, Jane."

Matthew smiled at Jade but said nothing.

"Thank you," Jade said. "But luckily, I'm completely fine. Matthew was...well, he really is the hero."

Laura beamed. "I'm so proud of him. He's *so* brave. You know there's a reporter here who wants to interview him?"

"Yeah..." Matthew shook his head. "He was very hard to shake when we came in."

"Of course, you're a local *hero*!" said Laura.

Matthew cleared his throat. "If you don't mind, Eric, I actually wanted to have a word with you."

"Not at all."

They stepped aside and Tiffany stuck her hand out. "Hi, I'm Jade's sister, Tiffany. It's nice to finally meet you."

"And you as well! I love your dress. And yours too Jade!"

Jade absentmindedly looked down at herself. She almost forgot what she was wearing – it did look really nice. Despite her left foot being slightly numb, she was once again glad that she wasn't in the frumpy outfit. "Thanks!"

"Is that a Fritz Brique?" Laura asked, reaching out to touch the fabric of Jade's dress.

Tiffany nodded. "Yep."

Laura gasped. "It's *so* beautiful. I've never seen one in person before."

Jade shot Tiffany a look and mouthed "Fritz Brique?" But Tiffany was determined to ignore her and keep smiling.

"I think I'm going to hunt down another glass of champagne," Tiffany announced. "Be back in a second."

"Good luck," Laura said with a laugh.

Jade felt a sudden panic for being left alone with Laura. The silence hung between them for a moment before Laura broke it.

"I'm so thankful that Matthew got there when he did."

"Oh," Jade touched her hand to her chest. "Me too. I mean – I'm not exaggerating when I say he saved my life."

"He's amazing," Laura said with a smile. "You know, I'm really glad that I decided to give us another chance. After the whole, you know, incident."

"Oh definitely." Jade nodded, trying to figure out what she was talking about.

Laura tilted her head, smile frozen on her face. "Did he tell you about that?"

Jade took a big sip of her soda. "Oh I'm sorry, what?"

"The cheating."

She shook her head. "No, I'm uh – "

Laura's smile brightened. "It was nothing, really. How could I ever fault him? He's a dream."

Jade nodded. She felt like she had a stupid smile stuck on her face but didn't know what else to do. "You guys make a great couple."

"Thank you! You're too sweet. Well," she said with a sigh, "I think he owes me a dance. Have a great rest of your night!"

"You too!"

Jade needed to sit down. She had no idea what had just happened; all of a sudden she felt sweaty and too hot.

"Whoa, are you okay?" asked Tiffany, returning with two glasses of champagne. "I was trying to find Sidney to harass him a little but the man is nowhere to be found. Anyway, I got you a drink."

"What's the point?" Jade said, crossing her arms. "We don't have a chance. This party is amazing. They have a ton of money and support and they're going to beat us. Unless someone kills me first, then I'll be dead *and* they'll beat us."

"Oh come on," Tiffany said gently. "You don't believe that."

"I just...I think I want to go home."

"Okay! You don't have to tell me twice. This champagne isn't even good anyway."

Jade turned and pushed her way to the door. She couldn't spend another moment in there.

Chapter 17

Finally, Margie had her chance.

She'd spent weeks waiting for this. It was unfortunate, then, that it happened to be on a Tuesday when Hank asked if she'd like to get lunch. It was rare that he'd have time during work to do that, so she usually jumped at the opportunity. But now she had to make up an excuse as to why she couldn't.

"I'm sorry honey, I actually have some clients coming to see the barn. They're planning...an anniversary party."

"Oh? Anyone that I know?"

"Nope, I don't think so. They live in Burlington."

"And they're making the trip out here today just to see the barn?"

Margie swallowed. "Yep!"

He stared at her for a moment. "Huh, weird. Alright, good luck with that. I'll see you tonight?"

"Of course!"

She hated fudging the truth, but she had no choice. It wasn't a *complete* lie – there *was* someone coming to see the barn for an anniversary at some point that week. She needed to keep her real plans private...for now.

Hank was the Chief Deputy Sheriff, after all. If he knew what she was up to, he'd be obligated to stop her. Or worse – if she got caught, and it came out that he knew what she was doing...well, that would just be too terrible. It could ruin his career. It would ruin his credibility.

Margie just had to make sure that she wasn't caught.

When all of this craziness started, Margie had to make excuses to go over to Jade's house to check on her. After Jade's car was broken into, Margie liked to stop by any chance she had; she just needed to make sure that Jade was okay. But then Morgan and Hank started teasing her, so she had to be more sneaky about it. Whenever she ran an errand, she'd stop on the way there or on the way home.

Nothing crazy – she might drive past Jade's house once or twice a day to make sure that nothing unusual was going on. Sometimes she'd pop in to say hello, and sometimes she'd just sit outside for a bit. And after the house was broken into, sure, maybe some of her errands were unnecessary, but who cared? Hank only asked her once why it took her an hour to get milk, and when she told him she'd "swung by" Jade's, he stopped asking questions.

She knew that it sounded crazy, but she had a terrible feeling about it all. From the very beginning, Margie was terrified that something bad was going to happen to Jade.

But Jade refused to even talk about it and made excuses for everything that happened. She even brushed off the threat at the barn!

What could have been clearer?

That was Jade's way though – she never made a fuss. But not Margie. She'd been around long enough to know that some situations *required* a fuss. And sometimes, the biggest disservice a woman could do to herself was to keep quiet when her heart told her to speak up.

The threat after the fundraiser was the last straw for Margie. She was done keeping quiet. On the night of the fire, she was actually on her way to Jade's to have a serious talk.

Margie didn't have to sneak out of the house that night; Hank was busy catching up with some friends, so all she had to do was get in her car and rehearse the speech she'd planned. She was almost to Jade's house when another car blew through a stop sign and T-boned her car.

Her first reaction was shock – did that really just happen? When she realized that she wasn't hurt, she was about to get out of the car and check on the other person. But instead of extending the same courtesy, the other driver spun around and drove off in the other direction!

That made Margie even *more* shocked! She called the police, hoping that maybe they could catch whoever this person was, driving around with a damaged car. But when she was waiting, she got the news about the fire, so instead she abandoned her car and rushed off to the hospital.

It wasn't until a few days later that she even thought about her car again. Hank pressed her for details to see if she could remember anything about the person that hit her, but frustratingly, it was like her memory was wiped clean.

It was only when she went to pick her car up from her mechanic John that she got a clue. It started the way that all good gossip starts.

"You know, I really shouldn't be saying this..." he said, scratching the back of his neck.

Margie leaned in closer. "But?"

He sighed. "But you said that you still didn't know who hit you, right?"

"Right."

"Well I can't say for sure, but a buddy of mine came in here with his car busted up. He said he hit a deer – but I'm not so sure."

Margie raised an eyebrow. "Interesting. And this buddy was...?"

"Eddie. Eddie Mills. Do you know him?"

"*Everyone* knows Eddie," Margie said with a sigh. "I made the mistake of hiring him to do some work for me once."

John laughed. "Yeah, that's Eddie. I don't know for sure that he was the one that hit you. But he came in the next day all in a frenzy. Said that he needed the car fixed but he was leaving the island for a while."

"Why?"

John shrugged. "I'm not sure. But I knew that he left some jobs unfinished."

While it wasn't unlike Eddie to leave his work undone, the whole situation made Margie suspicious. If he was the one who hit her, why was he speeding through the night like that to begin with? And he just *happened* to be coming from the direction of Jade's house? And then, for some reason, he had to flee the island?

Every time she thought about it, all she could see was Eddie's smug face, stuffed with hors d'oeuvres at the fundraiser. She thought he was up to something then, but now...

Now she was *sure* he was up to something.

"Do you know who he was working for? Maybe I'll stop in and pay him a visit, see how his car is doing."

John put his hands up. "I can tell you, but remember – you didn't hear anything from me."

Margie smiled. "My lips are sealed."

John told Margie about the handful of jobs he was aware of. The biggest one was an addition to a new restaurant near Roche Harbor. Luckily, Margie knew the owner and was able to stop by and ask how things were going.

"Terrible!" Betty said. "He disappeared without a trace."

"That's how he was when I hired him," Margie said. "It took a lot of convincing to get him to finish the job."

"Let me know if you see him so I can get on his case."

Margie nodded. "Would you mind giving me a call, too, if you see him first? I need to talk to him about something."

"Sure."

And that was the call that came in on Tuesday – two weeks later. Apparently, Eddie returned from his mysterious trip and started making promises about when he'd finish the various jobs. He did good work – when he was in the mood. Margie had found much better contractors since she'd worked with Eddie, but poor Betty was just discovering how flighty he could be.

"Don't tell Eddie that I'm coming," Margie said when she got the call. "I'd like to surprise him."

As she drove north, Margie didn't feel nervous at all. She only felt determined. It was better that no one knew what she was up to – explaining it would've made her sound a bit crazy. And it was good that Hank didn't know, because he surely would've tried to talk her out of it.

There was no going back. She pulled up to the restaurant and saw Eddie right away. It looked like he had two other guys working with him. He alternated between being on his phone and yelling orders.

This was going to be harder than she thought. She got out of her car and approached him; as she got closer, he saw her before turning his back to her, continuing his phone conversation.

Margie didn't mind. She stood next to him, waiting until he finally had to get off the phone.

He said his goodbyes before turning around. "Margie, how's it going?"

"You tell me Eddie. How's your car?"

He shrugged. "Just fine. Why do you ask?"

Margie narrowed her eyes. "I heard you had some trouble with it."

He set his phone next to his toolbox and frowned. "Nope. No trouble here. Is there something I can help you with?"

Margie smiled and casually leaned her weight onto a nearby ladder. "Well – "

"Watch it!" Eddie yelled. The ladder came crashing to the ground, trailed by a small can of paint.

"Oh my goodness!" Margie covered her mouth with her hands. "I am *so* sorry Eddie."

"You come around here poking your nose into my business, making a mess? Get out of here!" he yelled, stooping to flip the paint can right side up and collect the brushes that scattered in the grass.

"I'm such a klutz," Margie said. "And you're obviously busy, I'll talk to you later."

"Yeah, yeah." He didn't look back at her, instead focusing on cleaning up the mess she'd made.

She felt bad about the spilled paint – that wasn't nice of her. But it was a price she was willing to pay.

Margie turned and walked back to her car, trying to act natural – but all she could think about was Eddie's phone, tucked snugly into her coat pocket.

Chapter 18

His phone vibrated. Again.

Matthew closed his eyes, letting out a sigh. He'd asked Laura to stop calling him while he was at work, but she'd already called twice that day.

The first time was because he hadn't answered her text about going to the country club to finalize their membership. The second time, she was eating lunch and was bored.

If she was calling about the country club *again*, he wasn't going to answer. He didn't feel like getting into this argument right now.

Or ever.

He'd made it clear that he wasn't interested in joining – he'd even found an alternative group that they could join for a far more reasonable price: twenty dollars a year.

That suggestion didn't go over well, though. He first brought it up that past weekend. The argument lasted for *hours* and made them late for the party on Lopez Island. For some reason, their biggest fights always happened before they needed to be somewhere.

It wasn't a fun night, compounded by the fact that Laura kept him so busy that he barely got to talk to Jade before she disappeared. He was worried she might be angry at him, maybe for being late. Or maybe because he didn't give her any updates about arson suspects?

He didn't know. But he never got a chance to talk to her. She probably had somewhere better to be – she looked quite dressed up. Laura made a comment about how Jade's dress was "too much" for the event, but Matthew thought she looked lovely.

He had to keep that to himself, though.

The phone rang again. He was afraid that if he answered he might say something harsh, so he decided to let it go to voicemail. A few moments later, it rang a *third* time.

He sighed, pulling it out of his pocket. Surprisingly, it wasn't Laura calling – it was Margie.

"Hey Margie, what's up?"

"Oh hi! I'm sorry to bother you at work – but I didn't know who else to turn to. Do you have a minute?"

"Sure, what's going on?"

"If I tell you, will you *promise* not to tell Hank? I'm going to tell him myself, just not yet."

That sounded ominous. "Are you throwing him a surprise party or something?"

"Not exactly. Actually – no, it's nothing like that at all. But I think I know who's been terrorizing Jade."

Matthew straightened up in his seat. "What? Really?"

"Yes. Can I meet you somewhere?"

Matthew looked around. "Oh – of course. Do you want to meet at the station?"

"No! Hank can't know yet. Not until I get your opinion on things."

"Oh. Okay. Well then..."

"Do you know the dock where Hank keeps his boat?"

"I do."

"Can you meet me there? I'm driving over right now."

Oh boy. What was he even agreeing to? As though he had a choice.

"Alright – I'll be there soon."

"Excellent."

The line disconnected. Matthew laughed to himself – he'd never heard Margie sound like that. She was still nice, of course, but very no-nonsense.

It took him about fifteen minutes to get there, and Margie was already waiting. He spotted her standing at the edge of the dock. No one else was around, and the only other sounds were the birds and boats gently rocking on the water.

"It's very peaceful here," Matthew said once he was closer. "So I feel like I have to ask if you're going to murder me."

"What?" Margie chuckled. "No Matthew, I'm not going to murder you. But I might murder Eddie Mills."

Matthew had stopped a few feet from her and crossed his arms. "Oh?"

"Now this is going to sound crazy, but hear me out. On the night that Jade's house caught on fire, I was on my way over to talk to her when I got into a car accident."

"Wait a minute," Matthew held up a hand. "Did you call the police about that?"

Margie nodded. "I did! But when I got the news of the fire, I had to run. So I never really reported it, and it didn't matter, because the guy who'd hit me just drove away."

"I'm so sorry Margie – I think I was about to respond to your call, but then Jade's house – "

Margie waved a hand. "Oh please don't apologize, I'm much happier that you rescued Jade than dealt with my little fender bender. In fact, after I rushed to the hospital and spent the weekend getting her all settled in the new place, I kind of forgot about it. I don't really care about cars."

Matthew nodded. "Okay."

"But listen to this. When I picked up my car from the mechanic, he hinted that Eddie had some damage to *his* car that he thought was a bit suspicious."

Matthew sighed. "Who's your mechanic? He really should've told us about – "

"No," Margie shook her head. "I can't tell you, it's a secret. He didn't want to point fingers if he wasn't sure, you know? So I went to go see Eddie – "

"Uh huh. I see where this is going. I'm sure he just confessed to it all and apologized, right?"

"No – and I don't care about any of that. I don't care about the car. I mean – it wasn't a nice thing for him to do, but that's not the point. The point is, if he was the one who hit me, then it was really strange that he ran off like that. Eddie isn't a nice guy, but I don't think that he'd normally hit another car and then flee the scene."

"What makes you say that? People panic."

"Because," she said, her speed picking up, "last year he got into a fender bender with someone else and he made a big show about making sure their car got fixed and acting like he was this great guy. And everyone knows him, so it'd be hard to get away with something like that."

"Well – that doesn't mean – "

"And the more I thought about it," Margie continued, "the more fishy it seemed. He had some *pretty* nasty things to say about Jade's plan when she first went to the county council with her idea."

Matthew shrugged. "While that may be true, it seemed like he was in support of her at her fundraiser."

"He was lying, I *know* he was. He showed up and was being *so* nice – something wasn't right. And right after Eddie dropped off his broken car with the mechanic, he fled the island and left a bunch of work undone. I think that when he hit me – I *really* think it was him – he was coming from Jade's house! It all makes sense! The timing is right, the direction he was coming from is right, and – "

Matthew crossed his arms. "I'm happy to go and question him, but if we don't have any evidence, it's going to be tough."

Margie reached into her pocket and pulled something out. "Well...what if I told you that I had his phone?"

"Then," Matthew said slowly, "I would tell you that I'm not able to use any evidence that wasn't obtained legally."

"Come on, can't we just have a look? One time Morgan said that phones track everywhere you go. Couldn't we see if he was at Jade's house the night of the fire?"

Matthew looked around to make sure that no one was watching them. Margie was definitely taking a page out of Morgan's vigilante playbook, and Matthew wanted nothing to do with it.

"Margie, I really can't be involved with this. I promised you that I wouldn't tell Chief Hank, and I won't. But he would tell you the same thing. You need to get that phone back to Eddie and hope that he doesn't notice that you stole it."

"I didn't steal it!" she said. "I *borrowed* it. No – maybe I thought it was my phone in all that commotion when the ladder fell over."

Matthew pretended to cover his ears. "I don't know what you're talking about, and I don't want to know."

"I can't let him get away with hurting Jade!" Margie said, her volume rising.

"I know," Matthew said, softening his voice. "We're working night and day to figure out who's been doing all of this, and I hate that I don't have any lead suspects. But we can't just go around stealing people's phones and accusing them of arson."

Margie frowned. "Well, maybe *you* can't."

He laughed. "Right, I can't. Why don't you call Jade? Just to let her know how worried you are about her. Maybe tell her how many nights you've been sitting outside of her house, watching from your car."

Margie took a step back. "How did you know about that? Did Hank tell you?"

Whoops. Maybe he shouldn't have said that. But whatever – it was too late now. And maybe she'd feel better if she knew that he was worried, too.

"No," he replied. "Hank didn't say anything. But you're not the only one who's been checking on her."

Margie's eyes widened. "Oh. I see."

He looked around, already regretting his confession. "I just wanted you to know that – "

"So that night of the fire? Did you get a call?"

He cleared his throat. "Not exactly."

"You were just..."

"Yeah," he said. "I was just...checking in."

"But you didn't see anyone running away?"

"Not a soul."

Margie stared at him for a moment but said nothing.

Matthew felt uncomfortable under her gaze. "How about this? I'll call Jade and let her know what's going on. Maybe you can talk to her about your theory with Eddie and see if he said anything strange to her?"

Margie frowned. "Do I have to tell her about the phone?"

"I mean," Matthew said with a laugh, "that part is up to you. But you may need her help in getting it back to him."

Margie thought for a moment. "Alright. It's a deal. But only because I like you, Matthew."

Matthew pulled his phone out and dialed Jade's number. He didn't dare say it out loud, but he thought Margie might be onto something.

If only there were some way to prove it.

Chapter 19

"Guys! Come check this out!" Jade yelled.

Tiffany and Morgan appeared at her bedroom doorway.

"What's up?" asked Morgan.

"Watch this," Jade said. She told Toast to sit in the far corner of the room, then slowly walked towards the door, placing a treat on the floor.

"Stay," she said, backing away from the treat. "Stay there. Good boy. *Stay*."

Jade flashed a smile back at Tiffany and Morgan. Toast was completely focused on her. "Okay, go get it!"

Toast practically jumped up in excitement to run to the treat.

Tiffany and Morgan clapped, and Jade turned towards them, a smile plastered on her face.

"Congratulations on another great trick," Morgan said. "Next, I'd like you to teach him to open the fridge and bring me snacks."

Jade tapped her chin. "Hm, honestly I bet he could do that."

"So smart," Tiffany said with a sigh. "But so furry. If only he didn't shed so much."

"Aw, don't listen to her Toast." Jade pretended to cover his ears. "You're perfect just the way you are."

Morgan leaned against the doorframe, crossing her arms. "So would you say that today has been pretty productive for you, workwise?"

Jade laughed. "Not really. Can you tell?"

"I haven't been productive either," Morgan said with a shrug. "I'm just glad you're not moping around like you were this morning."

"I wasn't *moping*," Jade replied, lowering herself to the ground to pet Toast.

"You were," Morgan said. "So I'm glad that Toast could cheer you up. You've been depressed ever since you went to that party on Lopez. What happened?"

Jade kept her eyes focused on Toast, who was now playfully pawing at her. "Nothing."

Morgan turned to Tiffany. "Okay, what happened?"

"I'm not sure," Tiffany said. "One minute she was all cute and excited, and the next minute, she wanted to go home."

"It was just really hard seeing how we're going to have no chance. They have these really fancy parties and all this money..." Jade's voice trailed off.

"No." Morgan shook her head. "Nope. I don't believe that. That never got you down before."

Jade shrugged. "I guess the fire changed me."

"Aw," Tiffany shot Morgan a look. "Now you've done it."

Morgan shook her head again. "Nope. I still don't believe you. What happened."

Jade sighed. Why was Morgan so good at this? "I don't know. It's silly."

Now Tiffany's interest was piqued. "What's silly? Was it because we saw Brandon?"

Jade looked up at them. Toast was now completely laying in her lap, basking in the attention of the moment. "What? No. That didn't bother me. Not at all."

"He was oddly friendly," Tiffany continued. "I wonder if he was trying to cover something up?"

Jade shook her head. "Believe me, Brandon is *not* that sneaky. I don't think he has anything to do with what's been happening."

"Then what?" Morgan paused. "*Oh.*"

Tiffany looked at her. "What?"

Morgan dropped her voice. "Was Matthew there?"

Jade closed her eyes. "That's not – I didn't say that he – "

"He was! And he brought Laura," Tiffany said matter-of-factly. "They were super late. We didn't really talk to them much, though."

"What did you talk about?" Morgan asked.

"I don't remember, we all talked to that guy Eric. He seems like kind of a weirdo and couldn't get Jade's name right. And then – "

Jade interrupted. "You two don't have to act like I'm not here!"

Morgan smiled. "Then *you* tell me what happened. Come on – I'm not trying to make fun of you. Maybe I can help."

Jade crossed her arms, and Toast immediately started pawing at her hand. She uncrossed her arms and kept petting him. "I feel *really* stupid saying this, because it's not even any of my business."

Morgan leaned forward. "Oh! Gossip! Now you have to tell."

"It's not anything good. Laura said – and I don't even know how it came up – but she said that Matthew cheated on her. And I guess that's why they broke up last time."

Tiffany and Morgan looked at each other, then back at Jade.

"I know it's silly," Jade added, "but it kind of upset me. Because I really like Matthew, and I felt like...you know, that he was a good friend. And a good guy. But apparently he's been dating Laura, and what if this is sort of his thing? You know, to like...*cheat* on her?"

Tiffany burst out laughing. "I'm sorry – I'm not laughing at you. It's just – I mean, I don't believe it."

Jade cocked her head to the side. "What?"

Morgan nodded. "I'm with Tiffany. I have a feeling that Laura made that up because she can tell that Matthew likes you. And she's jealous."

"Oh come on guys, you're going to give me a big head. I mean, maybe he does kind of like me, because he's a scummy guy. He's a *cheater*. And that just makes me feel so...gross."

Morgan shook her head. "I just don't buy it. Matthew's not a scummy guy. But I've *always* thought he liked you. And if it's bothering you so much, why don't you just ask him?"

Jade laughed. "Oh, so you think I should just call him and be like 'Hey your girlfriend mentioned that you cheated on her, what was that about? And on an unrelated note, do you like me?' "

"Okay, not *just* like that," Tiffany said. "But I think you could bring it up somehow."

Jade was about to respond when her phone rang. She reached into her back pocket to dig it out and gasped. "It's Matthew!"

"Answer it!" Morgan said.

Jade's stomach dropped. What if she'd accidentally butt dialed him and he heard their entire conversation?

"I can't!" Jade whispered.

Morgan snatched the phone from her hand. "Hello, Jade's phone!"

Jade shot her a glare, then mouthed, "What does he want?"

"Yes, she's home. She's very busy working." Morgan looked up, listening to his response. "Oh – hold on, let me get her."

Jade tried to escape but she was pinned down by Toast. She had no choice but to take the phone. "Hello?"

"Hey Jade, it's Matthew. I don't mean to interrupt your work day, are you busy?"

There didn't seem to be any anger in his voice. Maybe he *hadn't* heard their entire conversation about him possibly being a cheater. "Not really – I was just taking a break to teach Toast a new trick. What's going on?"

"Well, I ran into your mom today and – nothing is wrong – but I was thinking that maybe you two should have a talk. She's...got some ideas about who our main suspect could be."

"Oh?"

Matthew laughed. "It's hard to explain. But I made this phone call to force her to go over and talk to you. But I also can't really be involved."

"Okay..." Jade said slowly. "Is something going on?"

"Let's just say that I need you to help prevent your mom from pulling a Morgan."

"Pulling a Morgan?"

"You know, taking the law into her own hands."

Jade smiled. "Oh. I got you. Yeah, sure – is she there now?"

"Yeah, one second. Let me get her."

A moment later, her mom was on the line. "Hi honey, I don't want to bother you, but – "

"Mom, did you get yourself arrested?"

"No! Of course not. Matthew just thought that...well I don't know what he thought."

"Do you want to stop by? We're all just kind of hanging out right now."

"Are you sure? I don't want to be a bother."

"Mom, you are *never* a bother. Please come over!"

There was silence for a moment before she responded. "Okay, if you insist. Hang on, here's Matthew."

Matthew cleared his throat and got back on the phone. "Hey, I'm sending her over. And if anyone asks – I was never here."

Jade laughed. "Got it. Thanks Matthew."

"Take care – I'll see you later."

As curious and concerned as she was about what her mom was up to, Jade felt oddly lighter as she hung up the phone. She'd never even considered that Laura would lie about cheating. And if Matthew wasn't a cheater, that meant he could still be a decent guy. That meant...well, at least they could still be friends.

Chapter 20

Margie parked in front of Jade's house, hesitating before getting out of the car. Matthew didn't seem sold by her theory – and now, she'd have an even tougher audience with both Morgan and Tiffany involved. Maybe she should just wave, say hello, and run back home?

But then there was still the issue of Eddie's cell phone. Couldn't she just throw it away?

No – that was a real criminal move. Disposing of the evidence. She didn't know what had gotten into her, but now she had to deal with the consequences. Matthew was right in saying that she was pulling a Morgan.

Truth be told, Margie now felt that she really understood all of the things that Morgan did in trying to find her mom's killer. Though she was *never* a violent woman, if anyone so much as harmed a hair on Jade's head – well, Margie didn't know what she would do. Apparently, she was capable of stealing!

She let out a sigh and decided to go in and confess her crimes. When she knocked on the door, all three girls answered, eager and intrigued by whatever excitement she'd stirred up.

They sat down in the living room and Jade made tea for everyone. She also put out some freshly baked cookies – it was quite nice, except for the fact that Margie now had to lay bare all of her sins.

After two cookies and a sip of tea, she took a deep breath and told them everything – well, except for the fact that

Matthew knew about the fire because he, too, was monitoring Jade's house. Margie herself didn't know what to make of it. She thought she couldn't love him any more than she already did – but there it was.

And now...well, she thought it best to tell Jade this detail in private. It seemed too important to mix with the rest of this.

When she finished telling her story, she sat back and took a sip of her tea. "Alright, now you can all laugh at me and tell me how crazy I've been."

"You're not crazy Mom," Jade said gently. "I just can't believe that you *actually* stole Eddie's phone."

"I think it's great!" Morgan said. "Now where is it? I have a feeling that Eddie doesn't know how to turn off the setting that would track his every move."

"Morgan!" Jade sat up. "I don't think we should do that."

Morgan shrugged. "Why not?"

"Well," Tiffany said, leaning forward, "what exactly are we going to do with that information?"

"That's a good point," Morgan said. "You see how hard the entire legal process has been with my mom's killer, and we *actually* have evidence. And a confession! So it'll probably be pretty hard to prove his guilt no matter what we find."

Margie sat silently, sipping on her tea, her head shooting left and right between them as though she were watching a ping-pong match. "You don't think that they'll be able to arrest him for it?"

Morgan sighed. "Probably not. Like Matthew said, they won't be able to use the phone as evidence."

"Where is it, Mom?" asked Tiffany. "Do you have it with you? Or did Matthew take it?"

"Oh no, I have it," she said. "Matthew made it clear that he couldn't be involved, for obvious reasons."

Jade laughed. "This is crazy! I can't believe we're even discussing this."

"Think about it though," Morgan said. "I think I'd feel a little bit better if I knew it was just Eddie. He's an idiot."

"You know this guy?" Tiffany asked.

Margie nodded. "Everyone knows him. And he's not what you'd call a criminal mastermind."

"My vote is that we look," Tiffany said.

Jade rubbed her face with her hands. "This is a bad idea."

"I agree with Tiffany," Morgan said. "Margie – you're the tiebreaker. What do you think?"

She looked at all of the faces staring at her. Jade was right that it wasn't a good idea – but what if this could put them at ease, once and for all?

Margie reached into her coat pocket and pulled out the phone. "Morgan, let's see what you can do."

"Yes!" she said, accepting the phone. She turned on the screen and immediately frowned.

"What's wrong?" asked Tiffany.

"There's a password on here. I can't access anything."

Margie leaned over to look at it. "Jade, can't you do a computer trick thing to get past that?"

Jade laughed, shaking her head. "Not really. I'm not a hacker. I mean, I could have found his movement data if there wasn't a password, but I don't know how to get past it. And I'm not willing to try."

"So all of my sneaking around and thievery was for nothing?" Margie let out a sigh. She really felt silly now. Why hadn't she even checked if there was a password before she stole the thing?

"I wouldn't say that..." Morgan stood up and put on her coat. "Let's go pay Eddie a visit. Who's with me?"

"Morgan – " Jade began to protest, but Tiffany was already standing.

"Let's go Mom!" said Tiffany. "I can't wait to meet this Eddie character. Wait – do you think he's dangerous or anything?"

Morgan laughed. "Absolutely not."

After a moment of consideration, Margie added, "*Probably* not."

The three of them stood there, looking at Jade. She finally let out a sigh and stood to get her coat. "For the record, I still think that this is a bad idea."

"What's the harm in asking him?" Morgan said. "And we're all in it together!"

They drove up toward Roche Harbor and luckily it looked like Eddie was still working at the restaurant. Maybe he hadn't even noticed that his phone was missing?

The four of them got out of the car and started walking towards him. At first, he didn't see them – he was very involved in a piece of wood that he was measuring or cutting or something. When he finally looked up, he did a double take when he saw Jade.

The color faded from his face and in that moment, Margie knew all that she needed to know.

"Hey Eddie!" Morgan yelled. "Do you have a minute to talk?"

"Sorry ladies!" He called out. "I'm really busy here. Trying to catch up on some work."

He tried to walk away, but Tiffany blocked his escape. "This won't take long."

Morgan pulled his phone out of her pocket. "Are you missing something?"

Eddie narrowed his eyes. "Is that my phone? I've been looking for that."

"You should really be more careful about leaving it around," she continued, "*especially* because it gave you away."

"What're you talking about?" He took a step closer to her.

Morgan tossed the phone over to Jade. "Oh, you know, just the fact that you have an app on your phone that you like to use for directions. Did you know that app tracks *everywhere* that you go and saves that information for all time?"

Eddie's eyes grew wide. "So?"

"So, it told us exactly where you were the night that Jade's house caught on fire."

He opened his mouth as though he was about to say something, but instead lunged towards Jade.

Margie was ready. She saw him coming and already had her hand on the pepper spray in her pocket. Just like she practiced, she clicked off the safety and sprayed him right in the eyes.

Even Margie was surprised by how fast she was – he never got a chance to touch Jade. He collapsed to the ground, coughing and yelling.

Margie put the pepper spray back into her pocket. "Don't you *ever* come after my daughter again."

Chapter 21

Once the initial shock of what her mom did wore off, Jade collected herself and ran to get some water for Eddie.

She felt bad for him – as soon as the pepper spray hit, he was on the ground, writhing in pain and begging that they leave him alone.

"Please! I'll tell you anything that you want to know! I didn't want anyone to get hurt."

He repeated some combination of those phrases for the next half-hour until he was able to open his eyes again. Once he was somewhat back to normal, though, he didn't want to talk. He rather politely asked for his phone back and promised that he wouldn't cause any more trouble.

Morgan and Tiffany took it as a victory. Even her mom was convinced that Eddie was guilty – she said that she could see it in his face. Jade didn't disagree with them – but there was something that bothered her. Just the things that he was saying – like that he would tell them anything that they wanted to know.

What else was there to know? Either Eddie came up with that plan on his own...or he didn't.

When they got back to the house, everyone was giddy with excitement. Jade knew that she wouldn't be getting any work done for the rest of the day, and that was okay; she was actually quite ahead of schedule on all of her work projects. The group decided that they would get some takeout and finish out the rest of the day as a girls' day.

When it was time for her mom to leave, Jade walked her out to her car.

"I'm sorry that you've been so worried about me," said Jade. "But hopefully now you can rest a little easier?"

Her mom smiled. "I think I can. Now I just need to go home and confess to my husband what I've been up to."

"Do you think he'll be mad?"

Margie laughed. "No, not really. But don't worry about that. What matters is that you're safe. I really don't think that Eddie will be messing with you anymore."

Jade nodded. "I think you're right."

"And Jade honey…" Her mom paused, hand about to open the car door. "There's one more thing that I need to tell you."

"Do we need to pepper spray somebody else?"

She laughed. "I hope not. But I do have a few extra canisters if you'd like some?"

Jade shook her head. "Thank you, but I'm okay. I still have the other two that you gave me – somewhere."

Her mom nodded. "Alright, fine. But I do need to tell you something. It's about Matthew."

Jade felt her heart rate pick up but she forced herself to remain casual. "Oh?"

"When I told him my theory about Eddie, he really wanted me to talk to you. Especially because he knew that I'd been sitting outside your house some nights, just watching."

"Wait, you were? *Mom*!" Jade felt her heart sink. Her poor mother.

"Of course, I was worried about you! And apparently, Matthew was too."

Jade stood for a moment, trying to absorb that information. "I'm not sure – "

"The reason that he was there when the fire started – the reason he was able to save you – was because he was already sitting outside of your house. Now, I don't know if he wanted me to tell you that but...I thought you needed to know."

Jade felt a little dizzy. "Wow. I don't even know what to say."

"You don't have to say anything to me," her mom said with a smile. "And I know that it's none of my business. But if you feel even a *fraction* of what that boy feels for you – you need to tell him."

Jade closed her eyes. "I can't."

"You can. I know you can."

And with that, her mom planted a kiss on her forehead and disappeared into her car.

Later that evening, Matthew stopped by to pick up Toast and Jade felt newly awkward around him. She imagined herself accidentally saying something like, "Thanks for bringing Toast over, bye, love you. I mean – love him." So she decided to keep her mouth shut.

As luck would have it, Morgan was bursting with excitement and wanted to give him an update on their day. The only thing that Jade dared to add was a thank you for his help with her mom. She also asked if they should expect any charges for the pepper spraying incident.

Matthew laughed. "I wouldn't worry about that. It sounds like Eddie knew he was in the wrong, and he threatened you. Right?"

Jade was about to say no, but Morgan beat her to it. "Oh, definitely. Very threatening."

"Now I need to talk to Hank and see what we're going to do about him."

"Can you maybe wait on that?" asked Jade.

"Why?"

Jade bit her lip. "I just wanted some time to process it – maybe get some more information. I don't even know if I want to press charges against him."

"Well," Matthew said with a sigh. "That'll be up to the prosecuting attorney."

"Will it be a difficult case?" Morgan asked. "We didn't even really get a confession out of him."

Matthew nodded. "Yeah, that's true. But..."

"Well – just keep me updated," Jade said.

"I will. I can't do anything until I talk to people who are much more important than I am anyway," he said with a laugh.

Jade wanted to tell him that he was one of the most important people on earth as far as she was concerned, but she didn't dare. Instead she just said, "Okay."

The next morning, Jade offered to pick Toast up in the morning. She felt bad that Matthew had to extend an already long shift by coming to her house in the morning and at the end of the day.

Also, it worked well for her plan. As soon as she got Toast into the car, she drove straight for Eddie's house. If the sheriff's department and the prosecutor decided to start asking him questions or bring charges for the arson, Jade might lose her chance to talk to him. It needed to happen now.

She didn't tell anyone what she was doing. First of all, she didn't want them to worry and insist on coming along with her. As long as she had Toast, she knew that she would be safe.

And just to be safe, she also brought along a can of her mom's pepper spray. *Just in case.*

When she knocked on Eddie's front door, he answered bleary-eyed and grumpy.

"What do you want?"

Toast let out a low growl and Jade patted him on the head. "Hi. I'm sorry about him. He's mostly friendly. But I, uh, really need to talk to you."

Eddie shook his head. "Oh no – I know how this works! You're going to try to get some confession out of me. Well that's *not* going to happen! Just leave me alone and I'll leave you alone, okay?"

Jade tried to speak quickly before he shut the door in her face. "I'm not here for that. But you almost killed me. The least you can do is talk to me."

Eddie let out a sigh. "All I can say is that I'm very, extremely sorry about the horrible accident that happened to your house. I was glad to hear that you weren't hurt. And that I know whoever did it didn't mean to do anything but scare you, and that they called 911 right away with an anonymous tip about what was going on."

"I believe you," Jade slid her shoe into the doorway to ensure he couldn't shut her out. "But I know that there's more to the story."

Eddie raised an eyebrow. "Oh yeah?"

"Yeah," Jade said with a nod. "So can I please come in, just for a few minutes? I promise that I'm not trying to trick you."

"Then why did you bring that vicious dog with you?"

Jade shrugged. "Because I wasn't a hundred percent sure that you wouldn't try to kill me again."

He grunted and pulled the door open. "Come in."

He led her to the kitchen which was, unsurprisingly, a mess. "You want anything? Coffee or something?"

"No thanks," she said. She pulled a treat out of her pocket and got Toast to sit next to her. He was eager to sniff around the kitchen, but Jade didn't want him getting into anything that he shouldn't.

"So what do you want to know?"

Jade cleared her throat. "After my mom – you know, sprayed you."

"Oh I remember," he said, turning to put some bread into the toaster.

"You kept saying that you'd tell us anything that we wanted to know. What did you mean by that?"

"I don't know," he said with a shrug. "I was under duress. You can't take anything I said seriously."

"I just need to know if someone else is going to come after me."

He sighed and took a seat across from her at the table. "I don't think so. But your troubles are far from done."

A chill ran down Jade's back. "What do you mean? All we have now are the final presentations for county council, and then the vote. I thought after that I'd be left in peace."

He sat back, arms crossed. "Maybe, maybe not. You know – powerful people want you out of the picture."

"Who?"

He shook his head. "I can't tell you that. Because they're powerful people – you don't cross them."

Jade let out a sigh. This is probably where Morgan would threaten Eddie and say that she'd been recording the entire time.

But Jade didn't work like that. So far, this entire ordeal was handled by people other than her. And sure, maybe her denial stage went on a bit too long. But she was the one with the broken window, the burglarized house, and the fire. She was the one that had to deal with all of this – and she wanted to be the one to end it.

"Would you say these powerful people had the idea for… breaking into my car?"

He nodded.

"And then sneaking into my house?"

"Sort of – that was just to spook you. Not to steal anything, just to scare you off."

"And the fire?"

He closed his eyes and rubbed them with his hand. "Let's say powerful people wanted the heat turned up. And they used the phrase 'turn up the heat.' "

Jade sat back. "Wow. So what comes after that?"

Eddie put his hands up. "I swear I don't know! That really freaked me out. I don't want anything to do with it and I stopped taking his calls."

Jade narrowed her eyes. "Whose calls?"

The toaster popped and Eddie got up to fetch his breakfast. Toast let out a little whine, clearly expecting that some of it must be for him.

"I told you already that I can't say."

Jade watched him for a moment. He wasn't a monster – he clearly felt bad about what he'd done. It was a comfort that he didn't mean to kill her – he was an idiot, sure, but he wasn't a killer. She could work with that.

"Did you know that by the time that I woke up, my entire bedroom was filled with smoke? I could hardly see anything and I couldn't take a breath without choking."

Eddie flinched.

Jade stared at him for a moment before continuing. "If Matthew hadn't showed up when he had, I would be dead."

She sat back. Jade wouldn't break the silence – she was much more comfortable with it than most people.

"That's awful," he finally said.

"It was. But I'm still alive. And I'm not going to give in that easily. Will you help me?"

He paced across the room once, twice before tossing the crust of his bread into the sink, much to Toast's dismay.

"Alright, I'm in. What were you thinking?"

Chapter 22

As expected, Chief didn't think that they could do much about Eddie.

"Even if we got a warrant, what're we going to find at this point?" he said.

"Yeah," Matthew replied with a sigh. "And I'm disappointed I didn't figure it out sooner. Maybe we could've recovered some sort of evidence, at least with the fire."

Chief nodded. "Yeah, but it's long gone now. I don't fault you for it. We didn't have much to go off of – and Margie was a woman on a mission."

"Did you know what she was doing?"

Chief shrugged. "Not exactly. I knew that she was up to something – and I knew that she was spending a lot of time worrying about Jade, checking up on her, you know. It seemed like she didn't want me asking questions, though, so I let her do her thing. I trust her."

"Of course."

Chief continued. "She just followed her gut, really. And it sounded like she got Eddie pretty good."

"Yeah, I think so. He was still scared when I went and talked to him."

"Maybe I'll stop by too," Chief said with a laugh. "I can't believe he would do something as dumb as starting a fire. Actually – I *can* believe it. But, you know."

"Unfortunately, he's not dumb enough to make a full confession, or even leave anything at the scene of his crimes.

Though Jade didn't seem like she even wanted us to pursue anything."

Chief shook his head. "That girl is a lot like her mother. Very forgiving. But we can't just let him get away with it."

Matthew smiled. Jade *was* a lot like her mom – and he was quite fond of both of them. "Let's hope that her pepper spray aim is just as good – if she ever needs to use it."

"Agreed."

There were only a few days left until the vote on Proposition 16, and Jade happily reported that absolutely nothing unusual happened since moving into Chief's house. Matthew was glad that she could feel safe again – that was what he wanted all along. He was fairly convinced that Eddie was to blame for all of the shenanigans. Work went back to normal, and Matthew didn't have to feel so worried that something might happen to her.

There was only one thing that he didn't know how to handle – Toast's daily visits with Jade. Matthew didn't mind making the drive, and Toast loved the attention. In a few short weeks, Jade managed to teach him half a dozen new tricks. He was even starting to walk nicely on his leash.

But now that she was no longer in danger, Matthew didn't know if she still wanted to deal with him. He didn't want her to think that he was using her as a free dog trainer; but when he brought it up to her, she insisted that she didn't mind – she even said that she loved spending time with Toast and having his company throughout the day.

Laura wouldn't like that it was still going on, but at least for the time being it seemed like she was swept up in the excitement of Matthew being a "hero." The word embarrassed him – he didn't feel like a hero at all. If Jade knew that he'd been sitting outside of her house, she definitely wouldn't think of him as a hero. She'd probably just think he was a weirdo.

And running into the house wasn't a choice that he made – when he heard her scream, he just reacted. Nothing would've stopped him from going inside – even if it seemed like he wouldn't make it out alive. The thought didn't cross his mind, really. He'd like to think anyone would've done the same.

At least Laura was quite pleased with being the girlfriend of a hero. Matthew was just glad that she hadn't asked about the country club again. And that Saturday, she was having a girls' night with some of her friends from work. Matthew was happy about it; it gave him a chance to catch up with Luke.

Initially, Luke suggested that they take Chief's boat out on the water for a spin. Unfortunately, Chief was *not* on board with that idea. Matthew suggested that they could rent a boat, but Luke dismissed it.

"No no, it's just as well," Luke said. "I'm supposed to take a boating safety course that I keep putting off. How about we head to the brewery and chat? I need to solidify our friendship now that you're island-famous."

That sounded like a perfect evening to Matthew. It felt like he hadn't gotten a moment's rest since the fire. Plus, the brewery was one of his favorite places on the island – it was a beautiful, brand-new building with warehouse tall ceilings and wide windows. There was a nice outdoor patio, too.

Once the weather was a bit warmer, he hoped that he'd be able to bring Toast onto the patio and relax with friends. It wouldn't have been a possibility before Toast attended Jade's obedience school – he would've been terrified by all the people – but it seemed that every day with Jade made him less fearful and inched him closer to being a confident dog. It was amazing to watch.

They met at the brewery and got a table tucked in the corner with an expansive window view. It was surprisingly cozy despite the open space being filled with voices and laughter. It felt good to be in such a lively place – it seemed like people were putting their worries aside for the evening, and Matthew felt the pull to join them.

They ordered a few things off the menu; Matthew sat back, enjoying the calm.

"I feel like I haven't seen you in ages," Luke commented.

"That's probably because you haven't." Matthew took a sip of his drink. "I'm sorry about that – things have been really wild since the fire. But how are things going with Morgan's case?"

"Alright I suppose. The trial is finally scheduled."

"No kidding! I can't believe I didn't hear anything about this."

"There's not much to hear yet. We'll see what happens once the jury is selected. I'm just trying to keep her occupied until then – luckily, work has been extraordinarily busy."

"That's good," said Matthew. "Have you fallen in love with weddings yet?"

Luke scoffed. "Hardly. But I don't mind it as much. Also, it was nice being able to make that video for Jade. People really seemed to respond to it."

Matthew nodded. "Yeah – it was great – really stunning. Much better than what Eric Burke is dragging around."

Luke laughed. "Thanks. I assume you'll be going to the presentations tomorrow?"

"I am – but I haven't broken the news to Laura yet. We're supposed to spend Sundays together, and she won't be happy about it."

"Ah," Luke crossed his arms. "You don't bring her around much. Does she not like us, Matthew?"

He laughed. "She does, she's just...having a difficult time adjusting."

"Right, right." Luke sat for a moment, staring into his glass. "You know..."

The waitress stopped by and interrupted Luke's thought. "Another round for you?"

"That'd be excellent," said Luke. "Also, I'd like to put in an order for those mini corndogs."

"Coming right up!"

Matthew crossed his arms. "Do you realize that you just charmed her so hard that she forgot to ask if I wanted anything?"

Luke frowned. "Sorry about that, but you really can't let this hero thing go to your head, Matthew. It's not always about you."

Matthew chuckled. "You're right. What was I thinking."

"I can't help it that those mini corndogs have been calling to me all this time. They shouldn't put them on the menu, they should just assume you want them the moment you walk in. There should be piles of corn dogs everywhere you look."

Matthew studied him for a moment. Luke wasn't usually this crazy about corndogs. This was new. This was...

"What were you going to say before she interrupted you?"

Luke shifted in his chair and shrugged. "You know, maybe. I'd heard a bit of gossip. From the girls."

Matthew smiled. "Is that what we call them now?"

He nodded. "Yes, as of right now. The girls. And Morgan is in charge, obviously, and I do think that she can be a *bit* exclusionary – and she may have been mean to Laura when she first arrived."

"I can see that," Matthew replied. "Not that Laura made much of an effort – she's trying to convince me to change departments."

"Like onto the mainland? Why?"

Matthew sighed. "She doesn't like making the trip out here. She said it's too inconvenient."

"I won't stand for it," Luke said, slamming a fist onto the table. "You're an island treasure and they can't have you."

"Don't worry, I'm not really considering it," Matthew said with a laugh. "She really wanted us to have a second chance though, so – here we are."

Luke smiled. "And how is *that* going?"

Matthew rubbed the back of his neck. "It's hard to say. I've been so busy investigating Jade's case that I probably haven't been very fair with my time."

"Right, so overall, not great," Luke quipped. "And as your friend, I can only assume, therefore, that there was a good reason why you cheated on her in the first place."

Matthew almost choked on his beer. "I'm sorry?"

Luke scrunched his eyebrows. "Oh – well, that was the gossip. Morgan told me about it."

"I never cheated on Laura. Is that what Morgan is telling people?"

Luke sat back. "No – that's what *Laura* is telling people. Apparently, that's what she told Jade."

"Well that's...interesting."

Luke put his hands up. "I'm sorry, I didn't really mean to get involved. I just have Morgan in my ear all the time, you know how she is, and I assumed that it was – well, that it was common knowledge."

"Apparently it is. To everyone but me." It seemed that Laura was spinning a narrative in her head – and nothing would convince her that it wasn't true.

"You know, I didn't really believe it," Luke continued. "Which is why I had to see your reaction."

Matthew laughed. "Thanks a lot Luke."

"Now that *that's* out of the way, we can go over the details of the video that we're going to make."

"What video?"

"The one of you running into a burning building. I've got big plans for you."

They both started laughing and the corndogs arrived. Matthew was glad that Luke told him about the rumor, but he didn't know what else to say about it. They moved onto different topics after he made it clear he wouldn't be starring in any fire reenactment videos for any reason.

The truth about Laura was more complicated than that – and further, it wasn't his secret to share.

On Sunday morning, Matthew was awoken by a call from Laura demanding to know which ferry he'd be taking to visit her.

"If you hurry, we might be able to get into this film festival. Apparently it's really up-and-coming!"

Matthew flipped over in bed. "I'm not coming out today."

"What? Why not?"

He reached out a hand to pet Toast, who was excited to see that he was awake. "I'm going to the county council presentations today."

Laura let out a long sigh. "Here we go again. You're always making me come out to you. And for what? Something really boring."

"It's something important. And I can't say that I'm terribly interested in a film festival."

"Matthew – I *swear*, if you do this again – "

He interrupted her. "Laura, I need to talk to you about something that I heard yesterday."

"What."

"Apparently my friends think that I cheated on you, and that's why we broke up before."

Laura was silent.

Matthew continued. "Now you and I both know that that never happened. If I remember correctly – "

"I don't know where Jade got that idea. I think she just loves drama – and I can't believe you even consider her a friend."

Matthew rubbed his eyes. "I never said that it was Jade who told me. It was Luke."

She was quiet for a moment, then said, "Oh."

He sighed. "What are we doing? Why did you move out here?"

"*Because!* I love you!"

"You love a version of me that would join a country club, or go to a film festival. Or move back home."

"What's wrong with wanting those things?" she said.

"Nothing. But it's not what I want. I haven't changed – I haven't – "

"I thought that if you moved out here for a few months, you could get it out of your system. And then you'd come back to your senses."

Matthew closed his eyes. "Does coming back to my senses mean doing the things that you want me to do?"

"Our life used to be good. It used to be good enough for you. What changed? What's so different now that you can't be happy with me?"

Toast whined, forcing his head under Matthew's hand. He needed to go outside – and Matthew needed to get on with his day.

And his life.

"Everything is different now, Laura. I'm sorry, but it's not you. I'm different. And there's nothing that we can do to put us back together again."

"Wait! Don't you *dare* hang up on me."

"I'm not hanging up on you. But I need to say goodbye. Things aren't working between us. We're both unhappy – again."

"I won't let you say goodbye. You just need to try harder, you just need to move back home and – "

Matthew gritted his teeth. Though it felt awful, it was more unkind to drag this out than to be honest with her. "I'm sorry, Laura. I wish you all the best. Goodbye."

He ended the call and then silenced his phone. He knew that there wouldn't be much peace today – that she would call and text and leave voicemails. But eventually, she'd stop.

And this time, he wouldn't be convinced to give up the life that he wanted for the life that someone else insisted he have.

Chapter 23

"Is there anything that we need to bring?" Hank called out from the kitchen. "I can take it out to the car."

Margie popped her head out of the bedroom. "Just those cookies and pies that I have set out on the counter! And the serving trays – but I'll get those."

Hank, try as he might, would never be able to find exactly which platters Margie wanted to bring. She had a very specific idea in mind for how she wanted things to look, and it was just best if she handled it herself. His help with the cookies was more than enough.

She finished applying a dash of mascara before grabbing the platters that she needed. She was pleased to see that Hank also picked up the bag she'd placed next to the door – it had some cute little napkins, forks, and plates so that people could enjoy these treats during the presentations without making a mess.

Hank came back inside and took everything out of her arms. "You have to let me at least *pretend* to help."

"Pretend! You *are* helping. Thank you sweetie."

He nodded. "You're welcome love. Did I tell you that I talked to Eddie?"

"No," Margie stopped to look at him. "Did you send him my regards?"

Hank laughed. "I didn't need to. He was already terrified. And I guess we'll see him today."

"*What*? How dare he show his face at Jade's presentation!"

"Now honey, do I need to frisk you before we go to make sure that you're not bringing any weapons?"

He set down the platters and pretended to pat her down.

Margie wiggled away, giggling. She was very ticklish. "I don't have anything on me right now, but now that I know he's going to be there, maybe I should!"

"I don't think you have to worry about it. Half of the sheriff's department will be there. Including me – remember me? Did you know that Chief isn't just a cute nickname?"

Margie laughed. "Yes, I know. Alright, you've convinced me. I'll leave my weapons at home."

They carried the rest of the supplies out to Hank's car, which was running and warmed up, waiting for her. She loved all the little things that he did – warming up the car, replacing the glass of water on her bedside table...there were a hundred little ways that he showed her that he loved her. Love, it turns out, shined through in the small and quiet moments.

As she'd expected, he was neither upset nor surprised when he heard about her snooping and subsequently accusing Eddie. He was a *bit* surprised that she pepper sprayed him – but that was quickly replaced with admiration.

He insisted that she shouldn't get too big of a head, though; he'd known she was up to *something*, but decided to let her get away with it for a while.

Margie appreciated the trust they had in one another. It was a kind of love she'd never dreamed of having – one she sometimes couldn't believe was real.

But there he was – driving along, quietly humming to the music on the radio.

The county council rented a theater for the presentations and when they got there, Jade and Morgan were already busy setting up. After giving Jade a quick hug and kiss, Margie busied herself with setting up the table of treats that she had made.

"You know," said Morgan, eyeing the spread. "Some people might be above bribery, but not me. Margie, you won my vote."

"Oh stop," Margie said with a laugh. "Jade had *better* have your vote! How's she doing? Is she nervous?"

"About as nervous as expected," said Morgan, reaching out to grab a chocolate chip cookie. "But she's practiced a lot, and she's ready. Did you know that they're broadcasting this online so that everyone who can't come will get a chance to see it?"

"I didn't know that." Margie bit her lip. "Does Jade know? I think that's going to make her nervous."

"It was her idea!"

Margie smiled. "Of course it was."

Poor Jade was always terrified of public speaking. Even when she was in kindergarten, they had to practice for the entire week leading up to her show and tell days. She was just *painfully* shy.

It got a bit better over the years, but Jade was always hyper-aware of any errors that she made when speaking, and worried that people would remember them forever. Margie was worried that this presentation would push Jade over the edge – but even from afar, she looked calm and collected.

Maybe it would all be okay.

People began filing in, and Margie didn't want to disrupt Jade's concentration, so she quickly wished her good luck and took her seat. Tiffany joined her, giddy with excitement – or, as giddy as Tiffany got. Margie didn't know why she was so invested in this project, but it was so nice to have her girls working together. It was a shame that Connor didn't live closer, or he could've come to support Jade as well. He'd remembered to send Jade a text, though, which was a lot considering that he was basically living in the mountains right now as a tour guide.

Jade sat up on the stage at a table with Morgan; the county council members had their own table, and then Burke Industries had a table with several people who looked overdressed. Eric Burke himself was still weaving through the crowd, charming people, laughing as if he were making a new best friend every minute.

Matthew came in and took a seat next to Hank, and when Jade spotted him, it seemed like they locked eyes for a moment. Matthew mouthed a hello and waved, and Jade waved back with a smile.

Margie clutched the program in her hand. Had Jade said anything to Matthew yet? It was interesting that Laura wasn't with him...or was it? Maybe she couldn't make it. Maybe she didn't *want* to make it.

Or maybe...Matthew uninvited her. Every time Margie saw them together, she caught a moment of twisted anger in Laura's expression. It never lasted long, but it was there. It made her whole sweet-faced facade seem superficial.

Margie wouldn't get her hopes up. At least not yet.

The lights flickered a few times, and someone from the county council spoke, asking everyone to take their seats because the presentations were about to begin.

Jade was up first. After being introduced, she and Morgan approached the podium. The screen lit up behind them and Margie grabbed Hank's hand – unlike hers, his was dry and warm. She held onto him and stared straight forward, frozen in the fear that something may go wrong.

The presentation lasted thirty minutes. It got off to a bumpy start, because the screen wasn't working quite right at first, but as soon as Morgan corrected it, everything moved quickly. They made some sort of presentation that zoomed and swooped, cutting seamlessly into parts of the video that Luke had created.

Jade and Morgan alternated speaking, soliciting laughter and commanding the attention of the crowd for the entire time. When a round of applause broke out, Margie felt like she could finally stop holding her breath.

It was over, and they were absolutely brilliant.

They took their seats and Eric Burke stepped up. He commanded the podium himself, and his presentation came off much more like a sales pitch. It wasn't bad – he clearly had a lot of experience – but he didn't have the same heart as Jade and Morgan. Margie recognized that she was a *tiny* bit biased, but the crowd didn't seem to respond as well.

After his presentation was finished, there was a ten minute break before they'd take time for questions from the audience. Margie jumped up from her seat, eager to congratulate Morgan and Jade on their presentation. But when she got to the stage, Jade was nowhere to be seen, and Morgan couldn't account for her disappearance.

Margie told herself not to panic – that Jade probably went to the bathroom or the lobby and *wasn't* kidnapped or anything dramatic. She looked around for Matthew anyway – he was coming up to talk to Morgan now. Maybe Margie should enlist him early?

No, no. She was panicking. She passed by him, waving hello, quickly moving to the lobby to see if Jade was already taking questions there.

No luck. She was about to begin a search of the bathrooms when she heard a murmuring over the speakers; the crowd in the lobby quieted to listen.

"Listen man, I'm really sorry about how this all turned out."

Margie paused – that sounded like Eddie's voice. But why? She peeked into the theater – he wasn't on stage. Where was he that he was near a microphone?

"Oh yeah? You're sorry? Do you have any idea how much money I'm going to lose on this?"

"Jared, come on – things got a little out of hand, don't you think?"

"That's not how I see it. You had a job to do, and you failed. Miserably."

Margie froze – everyone in the lobby was silent now, straining to listen. Who was Jared again? Was he that young man from the county council who always wore a fancy suit? It sounded like him, his flat tone, his controlled voice...but Margie couldn't believe what she was hearing.

"Whoa – that was a mistake. I didn't mean for anything to actually happen. I was just trying to scare her, I didn't want her house to catch on fire."

"If you knew what was good for you, you would've finished the job. You would've made sure that she never caused us problems again."

Margie gasped. She spotted Hank from across the room – he was looking around, wildly trying to find where the voices were coming from.

"I'm not a killer," Eddie said.

"*Obviously*. I should've hired someone else. You couldn't even make it look like an accident. Get out of the way – there are far more important people for me to talk to, and I need to salvage your mess."

Margie looked back into the theater and spotted Jade. She was sitting on the stage with her arms crossed. She had a smile on her face.

Jared appeared on the stage and as soon as he got close to the podium, the microphone squealed. He stepped away, a look of horror coming over his face. He tapped the microphone that was clipped to his chest, the thumping sound echoing through the theater.

He looked up, his face waxen, as Hank and Matthew rushed to his side.

Chapter 24

Jared was whisked away by Chief Hank and Matthew; as they walked off the stage, Matthew shot Jade a smile.

Did he know that she'd set it all up? She hadn't told him what she was doing; she hadn't told anyone. Except Toast, but he was good at keeping secrets.

Hopefully she'd have a chance to tell Matthew about it later. It was a legitimate reason to talk to him...and Jade found that she was always looking for those sorts of excuses now.

She made a mental note to bring up her inappropriate feelings for Matthew in her next counseling session. Surely Greta had some technique to make it all go away? She always told Jade that she couldn't control her feelings, but she could control how she reacted to them. But now it felt like she couldn't even control that.

Jade tried to focus on the scene in front of her; as she sat on the stage, the volume of the crowd steadily grew. She spotted the other two council members – Frank and Angie – in the far corner of the room. They looked just as stunned as everyone else. According to Eddie, they were not involved in any way – and now Jade believed that to be true. Seeing the shock on their faces helped confirm it.

It took a while for someone to get back to the podium and announce that the question forum would be delayed. It elicited a few groans from the crowd, but before long, people turned to talk amongst themselves and the issue was seemingly forgotten.

Though Jade was disappointed that there wouldn't be a chance to answer questions, she expected that it might turn out this way. Everyone was still trying to piece together exactly what had happened.

Jade managed to keep her plan with Eddie entirely to herself. She felt guilty not telling her mom or Morgan and Tiffany, but she thought it would be better this way. It was a delicate thing and Jade wasn't even sure it was going to work – but miraculously, it did.

Part of the success was because Jared couldn't hide his growing anger. Normally, he was the picture of self-control, framed by a perfect haircut and a tailored suit. Jade knew it'd be rare for him to lose his cool...but he finally did.

The cracks in his demeanor started forming right after she and Morgan finished their presentation, and it got particularly bad following Eric's lackluster performance. Jared knew that he was at risk of losing, and he was *enraged*.

It was subtle, but Jade recognized it. She'd become an expert in the slight changes that betrayed a person's true mood – she had Brandon to thank for that. She'd spent years living on eggshells with him and she knew that even the curve of a brow or the length of a stare meant something.

Once Jared was angry, he moved much more quickly than his normal pace and left the stage. That was the moment she'd been waiting for – that was when Jade sent Eddie in.

And she was right. It worked like a charm. Jared's momentary lapse in judgment resulted in him taking his anger out on Eddie, and the entire town got to hear it.

It felt good that she finally did something on her own; she didn't feel helpless anymore.

Before long, her mom joined her on the stage, hands on her hips. "I thought you were kidnapped when I couldn't find you!"

Jade got up to give her a hug. "I'm fine, Mom. I'm sorry that I worried you. I just had to make sure that Jared's microphone was still on."

She pulled away. "So you knew about this?"

"Yeah, you could say that...I knew about it, planned it..."

Her mom gasped. "I can't believe this! I need to hear everything."

"I'm happy to tell you all about it," Jade replied. She couldn't stop smiling. She didn't know what Chief Hank would be able to do with the information – maybe nothing – but it didn't matter. *Everyone* on the islands now knew what Jared had done. Everyone knew the truth. And that was the most important thing to her.

Morgan and Tiffany joined them on stage, but it was starting to get too loud to hear each other. They decided to sneak out of the back of the building to avoid the crowd.

Once they returned home, Jade was able to tell them the full story of what happened with Eddie.

As expected, before she could even start, everyone scolded her for going to Eddie's house on her own.

"I wasn't alone," she argued. "I had Toast. And...I took the pepper spray."

"Oh good!" her mom said. "Now you see how useful it is! Okay, you can go on with the story."

She told them everything that Eddie had told her. Apparently, Jared approached Eddie early on in the process – right after Jade got the county council to agree that there needed to be a vote.

Jared argued that Jade's plan would be bad for all of the business owners on the island; he said that it would make more sense to allow developers to build something grand that would bring in more profit overall. Eddie bought into it at first, especially because Jared offered to pay him to scare Jade out of advocating for the vote.

"But as you remember," Jade said, "Eddie's attempts were pretty halfhearted. I wasn't even really that scared."

"I was!" her mom said.

Morgan laughed. "Yes, even when our house caught on fire, you weren't afraid – apparently it only angered you more."

Jade shook her head but couldn't help smiling. "It wasn't *quite* like that. And anyway, Eddie told me that he was trying to make another warning – it was supposed to be the word 'stop' made out of firewood. When he tried to catch it on fire, it got out of control."

"If I *ever* see him again..." her mom grumbled.

Jade held up a hand. "Please Mom. Don't be upset. He's really sorry about what he did – and instead of me being scared off, *he* was scared off. He told Jared that he was done. And Jared got really angry but he didn't think that I had a good chance of winning, so he didn't do anything else."

Morgan shook her head. "Thank goodness for Eric Burke's extravagant parties making us look like amateurs! Please, go on."

Jade smiled. Those parties *were* a morale killer. "Also, apparently Jared couldn't find anyone else to do his dirty work – thank goodness. And Eddie regretted that he ever did it – he even tried to give the money back, but Jared wouldn't take it. He wouldn't even speak to him."

Tiffany shuddered. "What a weird guy. I don't even know him, but he sounded so strange when he was yelling at Eddie. I mean you could tell he was mad – but he was also *so* cold. What a psychopath."

Jade thought for a moment. "I don't know that he's a psychopath. I don't think he should be able to get off the hook that easily. He's just...really greedy. Apparently, he was going to make a lot of money off of this. Not from Eric directly, so I'm not sure how and Eddie didn't know – but all he cared about was his own gain. He's really selfish. Once I heard the full story, I didn't care about getting Eddie in trouble."

Her mom made a tsk sound, and Jade went on. "Really – I didn't. He's kind of a fool for getting involved, but he's not as bad as Jared. So we came up with the plan of convincing Jared to wear the microphone on his jacket."

"Oh wait!" Morgan said. "Is that why you were being so weird about the microphones?"

Jade nodded, smiling. "Yeah. I bought them."

"No!" Morgan's jaw dropped. "All of them?"

Jade nodded. "Yeah, the theater only had two that clipped on like that. The ones that I got were remote controlled, so I could turn them on and off whenever needed. When I offered one to Jared, he took it right away. I think it made him feel important."

"Wow." Morgan sat back. "Nice work on that."

"Thank you," Jade replied. Truth be told, she was quite pleased with herself. It went even better than she expected – there were about a hundred things that could've gone wrong, but they didn't. "I had to slip the audio guy twenty bucks so he'd help me set them up, and so that he'd keep the speakers on during the break."

"You thought of everything!" her mom said. "I'm just so impressed with you honey. Not just for catching this creep –

but for your presentation! We didn't even get to talk about how impressive it was."

"Oh – thank you," Jade replied, looking down.

"We *did* do a great job," Morgan said. "I can't believe that we were ever worried that we would lose. How can anyone vote for their idea over ours?"

Jade sighed. "There are still a lot of reasons why people may prefer the other plan over ours. But I think that we did everything we could, and there's nothing more we can do."

"Except," her mom said, "you *could* have let me in on this so I could have pepper sprayed Jared as well."

They all started laughing.

Jade shook her head – as satisfying as a pepper spraying was, this was even better. Whatever career Jared imagined for himself in San Juan was now certainly dead.

"Now all there is to do is wait for the vote," Jade said.

"So are we still having the voting party at your house, Mom?" Tiffany asked.

She nodded. "Absolutely! I can't wait. Win or lose – you're winners to me!"

Jade and Morgan simultaneously groaned.

"That's very sweet Margie," said Morgan. "But if we don't win, I'm burning whatever building Eric Burke builds down."

Jade snorted with laughter. "That's like a tongue twister. Burning whatever building Eric Burke builds down. Say it five times fast!"

Morgan tried to repeat it but ended up twisting her words. Everyone except for Jade's mom was laughing; she insisted that they stop making jokes about fires.

Jade smiled. "You're right Mom. No jokes about fires. And no more fires. Morgan – we're going to have to win this the old-fashioned way."

Morgan cocked her head to the side. "You mean with our charm, good looks and great hair?"

"No!" Jade laughed. "With hard work and heart."

"Oh, right. Yeah, we have that too I guess."

"I guess we'll find out Tuesday," Jade said. She didn't want to get too excited, but she felt hopeful that they had a chance.

Chapter 25

The day of the vote finally arrived, and Matthew was lucky enough to have the day off. He was grateful for it, of course, but part of him wished for more time to question Jared. It wouldn't be easy – Jared lawyered up immediately, and they had to be careful with how they decided to charge him. Chief had the idea to grant Eddie immunity in exchange for his testimony, and Eddie made it clear that he was happy to take a deal. They had enough evidence to prosecute Jared for *something*, they just weren't sure exactly what would stick yet.

Right after breakfast, Matthew went to cast his vote in the special election. There were a few items on the ballot, but most important to him was Jade's cause. He had the highest of hopes for her, and it seemed like a decent number of people were coming out to vote. That was a good sign – probably?

The entire island was still abuzz with the scandal from Sunday's presentations. The fire was one thing, but finding out that it was essentially ordered by a sitting council member? Juicier gossip didn't exist.

Matthew tried to avoid talking about it with anyone, saying that he had to decline comment on an ongoing case. He was grateful that he could use that as an excuse – he didn't like to gossip. Even if it were true, it wasn't his style.

After voting, he went back home and picked up Toast to take him for a long walk. They were getting into the time of the year when the weather was occasionally and briefly perfect. Today was one of those days. The sky was a clear, impeccable blue and the sun was shining. Matthew decided to take Toast to the west side of the island to hike the trails around English Camp.

He adored the history about the camp and San Juan Island's sovereignty. Initially, both the English and the Americans believed that the islands belonged to them. As the story goes, tensions reached a boiling point when an American settler shot and killed a pig for eating potatoes from his garden. English authorities threatened to arrest him, and in response, an American regiment made camp on the southeast side of the island. One thing led to another and the English sent three warships, causing the Americans to position their cannons for attack. When the news of the escalation over the dead pig reached the respective leaders of both countries, they were horrified.

After some negotiations, both sides agreed to scale down and jointly occupy the islands until a decision could be made as to which nation had sovereignty. The occupation continued for twelve *years* until an international arbitration by Kaiser Wilhelm I settled the San Juan Island dispute in America's favor.

Matthew read a plaque at the camp and chuckled to himself. San Juan was once a tinder box in the so-called Pig War of 1859, where the only casualty was...the pig.

There were only a handful of other hikers that day, so Matthew and Toast took their time walking through English Camp. Matthew liked to stop and read the signs, especially those that had historical pictures – some of the structures were still standing. They were both eerie and strangely modern at the same time.

He tried to imagine what life would have been like then – was it lonely living on this island? Were the inhabitants of San Juan as enchanted by the beauty of the island as he was now?

From English Camp, they continued on a steep hike up Young Hill. When they reached the top, he found blissful solitude. He sat with Toast for almost an hour, enjoying the view of the islands and all of the tiny boats below.

He'd completely shut off his phone so he could enjoy the peace, and it was a wise decision. When he got back to his car, he had a few text messages and two missed calls from Laura.

He read the messages – it was more of the same, with her saying that he made a huge mistake and that they were meant to be together. She accused him, once again, of throwing away their future.

It was difficult for him not to respond, but he knew it was the only option. All they'd done since she'd moved out west was fight, and if he responded now, it'd only be more fighting.

He cared about Laura and he hated to see her hurting so much – but it just wasn't going to work between them. He couldn't give her the life that she wanted, and she didn't want to share a life that he wanted. He should've known that it wouldn't work when she showed up initially, and he should've stayed strong.

But he didn't, and it only caused more suffering on both sides. At the very least, he now knew that he tried everything he could. One day Laura might even agree with him – but probably not until she met someone new. Someone who wanted the same things that she did.

He went back home and took a shower before going to the grocery store. He wanted to make something to bring to the party at Margie's that evening. He felt bad that Margie always did all of the cooking – even if she insisted in doing so. He offered to bring an appetizer and found a recipe online for buffalo chicken dip. It seemed easy enough that he couldn't mess it up.

He bought all of the ingredients and was about to check out when he came across a display of fresh cut flowers. Maybe he should buy some flowers for Jade? He reasoned it would be something nice in case her side won the vote. And even if she lost – it would still be nice to have flowers, right?

But then he second-guessed himself. Should he get flowers for Morgan, too? She was a big part of the project. And what about Tiffany? He didn't really know her well, but she seemed involved after her arrival. That would be three bouquets, though, and then it'd be weird not to get anything for Margie – she was the hostess, after all.

He spent about twenty minutes debating what to do and eventually walked away from the flowers entirely. Instead, he picked up two cards – one that said "Congratulations," and another that said "Keep your chin up!" Both had cute dogs on them, so he suspected that Jade would appreciate either.

When he got home, he got to work right away on making the dip. Toast wandered into the kitchen, yawning but very intrigued by the smell of the food.

"You're going to have to wait, buddy. Yours isn't ready yet."

Toast sat down, directly in front of the stove, and stared at him. Matthew laughed. Somehow it felt like Toast knew that he was getting something. Matthew had saved a chunk of chicken for him and planned to make it as a little treat.

Once the dip was in the oven, he got to work on Toast's chicken. Toast tried his best to stay awake, but it took so long that he dozed off a few times. He'd had a long walk, after all, and no one could blame him for neglecting his duty of keeping his eyes on the chicken at all times.

When Toast finally woke up and realized that he was getting a treat, he stood up, shook himself off, and started prancing around in excitement. Matthew put the chicken into his bowl and Toast gobbled it down in a matter of seconds.

He spent a few minutes searching the floor for more food, but when that proved futile, he went to the living room for a more comfortable nap. Luckily he'd be pretty tired from his walk so Matthew wouldn't feel guilty about leaving him to go to the party.

Once the dip was done, Matthew decided to work on writing a message in each card. He wanted to be prepared for any situation, but he found it surprisingly hard to come up with what to say.

He ended up going online for help, and after a painful twenty minutes, he was happy with what he had. It was almost a shame that Jade wouldn't get to see both cards since he'd put so much time into them.

Just before it was time to go, he changed and made sure to pack everything into the car – the dip, the bags of chips to go along with it, and the cards. Toast was snoozing peacefully when he left, as expected.

Matthew was the first one to arrive and Chief greeted him at the door.

"Oh for me? You shouldn't have!" he said, accepting the dip.

Matthew laughed. "Yep, all of that is for you. Enjoy."

"Hi Matthew!" Margie yelled out from the kitchen. "Come in and have a seat."

"Matthew brought food!" yelled Chief. "Was he approved to bring food?"

Margie appeared at the door. "Of course he was! He offered to bring an appetizer. That was very nice of you Matthew."

"I hope it's decent – I've never made it before. But I *think* I can follow a recipe, so I guess we'll see."

"I'm sure it's lovely! And it smells great. Do I need to put it into the oven or anything?"

Matthew nodded. "I'm not sure – maybe just for a few minutes? To remelt the cheese."

Chief handed the dip off to Margie and she took the two bags of chips from Matthew. "I think I know where she wants these. She has these big gold bowls – "

"Not the gold ones!" Margie popped her head out of the kitchen. "I want the glass ones. You know, the ones with the bubbles painted on them?"

Chief made a face. "Yes?"

She shook her head. "Just follow me. I'll show you. Matthew – you can go ahead and have a seat."

"Okay – are you sure that there isn't something that I can help with?"

"If I can't help, you *definitely* can't help," Chief said as he walked away.

Matthew felt awkward sitting at the table by himself, so instead he just hovered around it. Every time that he heard a noise, he thought it was Jade arriving. His heart rate picked up and his skin felt cold, but every time, it was a false alarm.

After about ten minutes, the front door blasted open and he heard Luke's voice calling out. "Come one, come all, to the island vote of the century!"

He went to the front door to greet him and was surprised to see that Luke was followed by all of the other guests – Tiffany, Morgan, and Jade.

"Hey guys – good to see you," he said.

"Matthew, be a doll and use those big muscles for something," Luke said, handing him a large glass platter. "I was charged with caring for these cupcakes until we got here, and the responsibility is too much."

Matthew laughed, accepting the platter. "Where do you want these?"

"Hm, can you please put them in the living room?" Morgan said. "Half of the cupcakes are for if we win – and the other half are for if we lose."

"What's the difference?" Matthew asked, trying to peek under the cover.

"None of your business!" snapped Morgan, slapping the cover back down. "At least not until we know if we won."

"Got it." Matthew set the cupcakes down in the living room as instructed.

When he returned to the table, Luke and Morgan were teasing each other and Tiffany had disappeared into the kitchen. Jade was standing by, quietly watching with an amused look on her face.

Matthew took a deep breath. It was time to stop being a baby and talk to her.

"Hey Jade – I didn't get a chance to tell you how blown away I was by what you did on Sunday."

"Oh – thank you," she said.

"It wasn't just your presentation," he continued. "I mean – it was great, but what you did with Eddie and Jared? That was just – well, it seemed like you got your mom's sleuthing skills."

She smiled. "That's really nice of you to say."

"Where's Laura?" asked Morgan, hands on her hips.

"Ah..." Matthew looked between their expectant faces. "We've decided to call it quits."

"Like *you've* decided, or you *both* decided?" asked Luke.

Matthew smiled. "I decided. And – this is kind of awkward, but Luke made me aware of some gossip that Laura was responsible for. And since you're my friends, I think you should know the truth – I never cheated on Laura."

"We never thought you did. That was ridiculous." Morgan waved a hand. "And I, for one, am glad she's gone, because – "

"*Morgan*!" Jade said. "Can you at least *pretend* to be polite?"

Morgan paused for a moment. "I can, but it's really hard."

"It's okay," Matthew said with a laugh. Luckily Morgan and Luke continued bickering and Matthew was able to pull Jade aside. "I actually wanted to talk to you about something."

"Oh me? Sure."

Matthew cleared his throat. As much as he didn't like gossip, Jade at least deserved to know the truth. They were all his friends, but Jade felt like...something more.

Even if he'd never have the courage to tell her how he felt about her, even if she probably never *once* thought of him in a romantic way, she didn't have to carry a low opinion of him.

"I really need you to know something – and I normally don't tell people, but – "

Just then, Margie called out, "Dinner time!"

Chapter 26

No!

It seemed like he was *just* about to tell her something important. Her head was spinning ever since he mentioned his breakup with Laura, and this was only adding to her confusion.

When he first said that they'd broken up, Jade had to force herself not to react. It was kind of shocking, really, and though she was dying to know more, she could *never* ask. Part of her wished that Morgan would have pried for more information – but instead, she'd gone right to insulting Laura. Jade decided she'd have to talk to her about that.

Mainly though, Jade reminded herself that this breakup didn't have anything to do with her – and it *certainly* didn't mean that Matthew had any feelings for her. That was more silly, school girl thinking.

She scolded herself for being so inconsiderate; he was probably really upset about the whole thing and the last thing he'd want was for her to go and make a move on him.

But...maybe someday she could tell him how she felt.

Yeah, one day.

Jade took her seat at the table and accepted the plate of scalloped potatoes that Morgan passed over. She racked her brain for what he might need to tell her. Was it about Laura? But what else was there to say? Maybe it was related to Jared.

Oh! Or maybe he wanted to confess that he'd been watching her house on the night of the fire. That could be an interesting conversation...was there a chance that he'd tell her why he was out there? Obviously, he was right to be suspicious and stop by, because he ended up saving her life. But maybe...

No. Matthew was a professional. He probably didn't tell her because he didn't want her getting any ideas.

That made a lot of sense and the fluttery feeling in her chest died off. She needed to stop looking for any little hint that he may like her. She needed to just give up.

"It looks like we're starting to get some results from the vote!" Morgan said, looking at her phone. "Do you guys want to hear?"

Everyone simultaneously turned towards Jade. She was caught off guard – for the first time that day, she wasn't actually thinking about the vote. "Oh – sure."

Morgan frowned. "Looks like Eric is leading us right now. But they only have two percent of the vote in."

"Maybe we should wait a bit longer before checking again?" suggested Tiffany. "The polls aren't even closed yet."

"I went to vote this morning," Matthew said. "And it seemed like a lot of people turned out."

Jade looked up and couldn't help but smile at him. How diligent of Matthew to go and vote first thing in the morning. Luke liked to call him a Boy Scout, but it certainly wasn't a bad thing. He was sincere.

"That's really nice to hear," Jade said.

Despite the ongoing conversation at the table, Jade kept getting distracted by her own thoughts. She told herself to stop daydreaming about Matthew, but then she would end up thinking about the vote, and that made her nauseous.

She'd try to force herself to focus on the conversation everyone was having, but since she hadn't been listening, she didn't know what they were talking about.

It was a relief when it was time to clear the table. Jade insisted on manning the kitchen: rinsing the dishes for the dishwasher, packing the leftovers, and hand washing the larger bowls and pans. It gave her something to focus on, and maybe Matthew might come help and tell her whatever it was that he wanted to tell her?

But as soon as she carried her first load of dishes into the kitchen, her hopes in regards to Matthew were dashed. Morgan had the idea to roast marshmallows on the back patio, and Matthew was pulled into helping build the fire.

Meanwhile, Tiffany volunteered to be her partner in drying. Jade enjoyed the company, though she worried that she might never get a chance to talk to Matthew alone.

Everyone was busy trying to make a fire and s'mores station outside; Jade could hear their laughter carrying into the house. Once Tiffany and Jade carried in all of the dishes and were alone in the kitchen, Tiffany cleared her throat and said, "So I chickened out."

Jade turned towards her. "What do you mean?"

"I was planning to talk to everyone at dinner about something."

"What's wrong?"

Tiffany shook her head. "Well – nothing really. I wanted to ask if it would be okay for me to stay with you for a few more weeks...or months."

"Wow!" Jade handed her a large bowl to dry. "I mean – of course it's okay! But is everything going to be okay for *you*? Like with your job?"

Tiffany threw the dish towel over her shoulder. "That's what I wanted to talk to everyone about. I actually kind of... quit my job."

"Oh my gosh Tiffany! What happened?"

She sighed. "It's a long story."

"You love your job! Was it because you didn't get that promotion that you wanted?"

Tiffany shook her head. "No, I got it. Me and my friend Malcolm were both promoted."

"Did you just not like your job after that?"

"No, it wasn't that. It wasn't all that different, really. I mean, I got a raise, which was nice I guess. But I was working all the time. Not that *that* was any different."

"Did something happen at work?"

"Kind of. It was Malcolm – he got sick."

"Oh no!"

Tiffany nodded. "He was diagnosed with kidney cancer a few months ago. It was really aggressive."

Jade covered her mouth with her hands. "I'm so sorry Tiffany. That's awful."

"Malcolm and I – we started around the same time and we were always competing with each other. You know, in a fun way. We helped each other out, too. We both spent all of our time working – because the job was what mattered most. They made you feel that way."

Jade nodded. She'd never had a job like that herself, but Tiffany seemed to love it. She never had time for anything else.

Tiffany continued. "When he got sick, it was like...none of his hard work mattered. He ran out of paid time off really quickly, so he had to take unpaid time to be able to go to chemo and stuff. And then they fired him."

"Is that legal?"

Tiffany shrugged. "I don't know, probably not. But he was so embarrassed that he wasn't able to come to work that he didn't really fight it. He had no one to help him – no one to take him to his appointments, no one to even help him get groceries. He had to get chemotherapy by himself – I mean, I took some time off to go with him as much as I could, just because it was so..."

Tiffany looked like she was about to cry, and Jade felt the tears coming to her eyes too.

"Tiffany I'm *so* sorry. That sounds terrible."

Tiffany took a deep breath. "And he...well, he passed away. And everything at work went on like nothing had happened. It was like he'd given his entire life to the company and..."

A sob escaped from Tiffany and Jade rushed to her side. She was able to grab a paper towel to offer – it wasn't as soft as a tissue, but it was the closest thing she could get.

Tiffany accepted it and dabbed at her eyes. Within a moment, she regained her composure. Jade had never known her sister to be much of a crier, so this was a shock.

"Here I go," Tiffany said with a laugh. "I was afraid that if I talked about it in front of everyone that I would start crying. I guess I was right."

"It's okay to cry, you know."

Tiffany smiled. "Maybe. Anyway – after that, I just couldn't keep working there. I don't even know how I ended up where I was. All I had time for in my life was work. And poor Malcolm...I mean, none of it mattered. None of it."

"So it sounds like," Jade said slowly, "you're rethinking some things?"

"Yeah." Tiffany straightened herself up. "I feel like I got on the wrong path somehow. And I don't know where to go from here, but...I'd like to at least *try* to find a different way."

Jade couldn't hold herself back anymore – she wrapped her arms around Tiffany and squeezed her tightly. "You can stay with me forever for all I care."

Tiffany laughed. "That's really sweet Jade. But I won't stay forever – just, you know, until I figure some things out. I really love being able to spend time with you all. Do you think Morgan will mind?"

Jade shrugged. "Probably not, but we can ask her."

"I really like her. She's kind of crazy, but she's fun."

"Yeah, she's a good one. And we'll have a blast living together!"

"That would be nice." Tiffany rubbed her forehead. "And I have to find a way to tell Mom, too. Life really is just so short. We don't have the luxury of time."

Jade nodded. "Yeah..."

Tiffany studied her for a moment. "It seems like you've been doing pretty well though – starting over?"

"It doesn't always feel that way, but it's getting a bit better."

Tiffany nodded. "Well, I'm glad. You seem a lot happier. And I'm happy for you."

"Thanks Tiffany," Jade said. This certainly explained the change that she'd seen in her sister – though it wasn't something that she'd expected.

Jade packed away the last of the food and turned back to Tiffany. "Actually, on that note, there's something that I have to do."

Tiffany cocked her head to the side. "Oh?"

"Would you be able to distract everyone so I can have a minute alone with Matthew?"

A wide smile spread across Tiffany's face. "You sly dog! Of course, I'm sure I can figure something out."

"Thanks sis!"

Jade slipped outside and walked towards the crowd standing around the fire pit, flames happily crackling along the logs.

"Oh no Jade," Morgan said when she saw her. "Is this traumatic for you? I'm so sorry, we can put it out!"

Jade shook her head. "No, not at all. It looks nice."

"Okay good, because it took us forever to get it going." Morgan's phone went off and she pulled it out of her pocket. She looked at Jade and smiled before speaking again. "Alright Chief? Margie? And Luke? I need all of you to all come inside for part two of operation s'mores."

"I can lend a hand," said Matthew.

Morgan shook her head. "No, you're the fire engineer. I need you to stay here."

He laughed. "Alright boss, whatever you say."

They all left and Jade was momentarily dumbfounded. It was far easier to get everyone to leave than she expected. Well – with Tiffany and Morgan's help, at least.

She took a deep breath and stepped closer to the fire. "It looks nice – you guys did a great job."

"Thanks," Matthew said, stooping down to add another log. "Luke was starting to get impatient – he wanted to dump lighter fluid on everything and we had to spend half the time explaining why that was a bad idea."

"Sounds like he went to the same camping school as Eddie."

Matthew laughed. "I think you're right."

"There's something – "

Jade was cut off when Matthew started talking at the same time. "I wanted to – oh, I'm sorry, you go ahead."

Jade shook her head. "No – you first."

He smiled. "Okay, if you insist. Earlier I wanted to tell you the truth about me and Laura. It's a long story, and I don't want to bore you to death, so I'll try to keep it short."

"You could never bore me," Jade said.

He smiled. "Laura and I dated for years. After college, we both got jobs at the same engineering firm. She had this vision of how she wanted her life to be – everything was picked out, even the neighborhood where she wanted to buy a house."

Jade nodded. "Sure."

"But things never really..." Matthew sighed. "Well, nothing worked out like she planned. The house that she wanted was more expensive than we could afford. So even though we both hated the company where we worked, we couldn't quit, because it wasn't part of the plan. She wanted to live in this neighborhood where all of our friends lived, and it was really expensive. She wanted to have a boat, because everyone else had a boat, and she even picked out the ring that she wanted me to propose with."

"Wow." Jade said. "Was it...nice?"

Matthew laughed. "It was expensive. But I went along with it – I mean, I went along with everything. I wanted to make her happy, and she seemed so sure about what we needed to be happy. I know it sounds dumb, but I didn't really question it, you know?"

Jade nodded. "Oh believe me, I'm not one to judge an imperfect relationship. You met my ex-husband, right?"

He laughed. "Yeah, so...anyway. The night before I was going to propose, we were hanging out with some friends and people from work. And I walked in on Laura kissing this guy we used to work with."

Jade gasped. "No!"

"Yeah." Matthew shrugged. "She swore it was the first time anything happened – he'd always flirted with her and she let it go too far. She begged me not to tell anyone, and she begged me not to ruin the life we'd planned. But after that, nothing was really the same. I realized that all of the plans we had were *her* plans. But I couldn't even be mad at her for long. She was looking for something else because she was unhappy, too."

Jade studied him. He looked perfectly whole now, but obviously that wasn't always the case. "That all sounds...devastating."

Matthew shook his head. "It was actually one of the best things that ever happened to me. I didn't realize how unhappy I was until I could clearly see how unhappy *she* was. I quit my job, returned the ring, went to the police academy, and moved out here. I was free, for the first time in years."

"So when she moved out here..."

Matthew sighed. "Yeah, that was a surprise. And it was her idea. She thought that she could win me back. Laura's not a bad person, she really isn't. She just...I don't know, she's too afraid to face what she actually wants? And nothing had really changed between us – we were just as unhappy, but we were here. She wanted to force us into a mold that didn't make sense. We fought about joining this country club like every weekend. I don't even know what you do at a country club."

Jade laughed. "Neither do I."

He leaned forward slightly. "And that's the story. I wasn't a perfect boyfriend by any means, but I didn't cheat. I never even told my family or friends the whole truth. It would destroy her too much and endanger her career there. I just left. But...I wanted you to know the truth."

"I could never think badly of you. I mean, you have to know that. You literally saved my life – you're the hero of San Juan."

He groaned. "Yeah, I know. Too bad I couldn't have kept that private too."

She laughed. "I know. So does everyone back home think you're just this heartless loon who moved across the country for no reason?"

"Pretty much. But that's okay. And I'm sorry that I cut you off with my TED Talk – you wanted to say something?"

Jade nodded. She opened her mouth to speak but wasn't sure what to say. She'd gone over it a hundred times in her head, but could never find the words "I guess – well…"

She stopped herself and looked up him. He was staring at her intently with those beautiful eyes, a half amused smile on his face.

She took a deep breath. "I'm not really sure how to say this."

"You don't have to be scared of me," he said.

Jade studied him in the firelight – she wished that she could freeze this moment forever. For the first time all day, she felt like her thoughts had calmed down. She was completely at ease. She wasn't afraid of Matthew – not at all. In this moment, she wasn't even afraid of him knowing how she felt. He didn't seem like he'd be one to kiss and tell…

She stepped closer to him. "I need to tell you a secret."

He smiled. "Okay?"

"Can you lean down?"

He obliged and Jade took the chance – she threw her arms around his neck and planted a kiss square on his lips.

He didn't pull away – in fact, he kissed her back and wrapped his arms around her. She had a flashback to when he carried her out of the fire. It was a feeling of complete safety and awe – but this time, she was overcome with joy.

After a moment, she slightly pulled back. "That's the secret."

"I'm so glad that you finally told me," he said in a low voice. "Because I've been harboring the same one."

Some shouts broke out and Jade turned to look at the window – everyone inside was cheering. For a moment, she was afraid they'd been watching, but then she realized that no one was even looking at them.

Jade hid her face in Matthew's chest. "For a second there I thought we had an audience."

"Me too."

She closed her eyes and breathed in the scent of his cologne, trying to memorize this moment.

It didn't last long. Morgan pushed the window open and yelled, "Hey you guys! Get in here! They just called the vote!"

"And?" Jade asked.

"*Duh*, we won!"

Jade caught Matthew's eyes. He dropped his voice to a whisper. "Do we go in, or do we run off together into the night?"

Jade bit her lip. "I say we go in, have a victory cupcake, and *then* run off into the night."

He looked up, considering it. "Deal."

Jade got on her tip toes to kiss him on the cheek. "I'm glad we're on the same page."

Epilogue

After selling off almost all of her furniture, there wasn't much left for Tiffany to ship from Chicago to San Juan. She'd rented one of those shipping containers and had everything sent across the country. When it arrived, she remarked to Jade how sad it was that everything from her life up until this point was contained in a seven by seven foot box.

"Don't think of it like that," said Jade. "There's a lot more to your life than *things*. Plus it's nice not to be bogged down with a bunch of junk. Or a bunch of history. Trust me."

Tiffany smiled and tried to make the mental adjustment. She still felt like she was weighed down by a lot of baggage, but Jade had a good way of looking at the world. Maybe it would help.

The rooms of her old apartment were easy to empty, but in the rooms of her heart, there were many doors that she preferred not to open. For years she was happy to leave them closed and not think about them at all.

It was easy to tell herself that she'd spend more time with her family or take that trip to Paris once her job settled down. But work offered endless distractions, and she was eager to take them.

What a fool she'd been.

Now she felt hopelessly behind in life. She was only a stone's throw away from turning thirty and she felt like she had nothing to show for it.

She felt lucky, at least, that she had somewhere as charming as San Juan Island to escape to. Not only was it an enchanting place, it was also a place where she still had the support of her family. She didn't feel like she deserved it, but there they were – helping her unpack her stuff and letting her into their lives.

Everyone showed up to help unpack – even Matthew and Luke. To be fair, they were coming over anyway to prepare for the first committee meeting for Colby's land. Jade was actually nominated for an official committee this time, and everyone pledged to help. Tiffany was hopeful that her background in finance could prove useful, so maybe the last few years wouldn't prove to be a total waste.

"We need to come up with a name for our house now that we're all living here!" Morgan announced as she carried her first box inside.

"What's a nickname for a witch's den?" Luke mused.

Jade and Matthew laughed, but Morgan completely ignored him and kept talking. "We need to go to one of those painting classes and make a rustic sign with the name. And maybe one that says 'wipe your paws' or something. That'll be for Toast."

"He can't read...yet." Matthew said. "But I'm sure Jade could teach him. She's taught him pretty much everything he knows."

Jade smiled but said nothing – she kept diligently carrying boxes and other odds and ends into the house.

Tiffany couldn't believe that she'd been so selfish that she hardly noticed her own sister being madly in love with the guy that saved her life. *Obviously* that made a lot of sense – Matthew was a good looking guy, and he seemed kind and attentive.

And he *literally* carried Jade out of a burning house.

Tiffany *really* should've picked up on that sooner – she should've had the sisterly insight to talk to Jade and see how she was feeling. But she didn't. She was too preoccupied with her own thoughts and problems.

She'd spent so much time on her own that she forgot that other people lived their lives and experienced normal feelings. Admittedly, part of that was because for so long, she had suppressed her own feelings and rejected anything inconvenient.

She didn't really know how to get back to normal, but getting to live with Jade and Morgan was a start.

Morgan returned to carry a lamp inside and continued her theory on the house. "We're going to be like the Three Musketeers! No wait – this is even better – like the three bears!"

That made Tiffany laugh. "How are we like the three bears?"

"I'm not sure. Maybe Luke can be Goldilocks? You know, coming around and complaining that nothing is quite right."

"It's not my fault that I like things a certain way," Luke said. "And Matthew – how about you show us all how strong you are and carry three boxes at once, eh?"

"Oh, do you want to race?" Matthew said with a smile.

Luke picked up a box. "Yes, you get those three and I'll get this one."

Morgan squinted at it. "Does that say pillows? Luke, you can't be serious."

"I have a bad back!" he yelled over his shoulder, slowly making his way into the house.

"He's the worst," Morgan said, shaking her head. "But also, the best. Don't tell him I said that."

Tiffany smiled. "I won't."

"You haven't found a job yet, have you?" asked Morgan.

"No," Tiffany shook her head. "I don't know what to even look for. Why, am I already behind on rent?"

Jade laughed. "No, I told you, Chief won't take rent from us. Morgan is just trying to con you into – "

"Ah ah!" Morgan yelled. "Let me tell her. Hey Tiffany, are you busy?"

Tiffany knew that she was about to get volunteered for something unpleasant – in the past, she would've had an excuse. But she'd decided to start saying yes to things to see where it took her. "Not at all. And I won't be for a while, I'm guessing."

"So...would you want to come with me to Andrea's trial?"

"Oh!" That was actually a lot more interesting than she expected. "I would love to."

"Really? It's a lot of sitting and waiting. They still need to do jury selection. And I'll probably cry a lot."

"That's perfectly okay," Tiffany said. "I would love to come."

"Great! I'll send you the dates!"

Everything was inside the house in record time. Tiffany didn't know where to put everything, and part of her wondered if she should just keep most of it packed up so she could move when she figured out what to do with herself.

She decided to ignore it all for now so that she could get involved in the first committee meeting. Jade baked blueberry scones and they smelled heavenly. Tiffany just wanted to run out and get one more look at the shipping container to make sure nothing was forgotten.

It was empty, as expected. Her moving crew was efficient, cheerful and best of all, free. When she turned to go back into the house, she saw that there was an envelope taped to the door.

"That's odd," she said to herself, taking it inside. She found Jade in the kitchen. "Hey Jade – I don't know how long this was taped outside, but I guess we missed it because the door was open."

Jade frowned. "Did you open it?"

"Not yet." Tiffany ripped the envelope; inside was a sheet of paper with a single phrase typed out: *It didn't end with Jared. Please be careful.*

Tiffany held the letter in her hand and reread it a couple of times.

"What is it?" asked Jade as she pulled the scones from the oven.

"Uh – I think we have a problem."

Jade studied it carefully before saying, "Well that's not good."

Tiffany shook her head. "No. It isn't."

"Mom is going to freak out."

Tiffany laughed. "Is that the first thing you think of? Not that someone's going to try to burn this house down?"

"No," Jade said with a shrug. "I wouldn't say that was my *first* thought. This person seems like they're trying to warn us, not threaten us."

Tiffany closed her eyes. "Oh great, here we go again!"

Jade stuffed the envelope into her her back pocket. "We figured it out once, and I'm sure we can figure it out again. Let's go, everyone's waiting for us."

"That's it?" She wasn't used to her sister being so...confident. This was a side of Jade that she didn't know – but one that she liked quite a lot.

Jade smiled. "C'mon big sis! Don't tell me you're afraid of a little local politics."

"I'm glad you feel that way." Tiffany paused. She had to admit – it *was* kind of exciting. "Where's the pepper spray?"

"That's the spirit!" Jade said as she walked into the living room.

Tiffany laughed. At least she wouldn't have to worry about life being boring on this little island. She grabbed the teapot and a stack of mugs before following Jade into the other room.

Introduction to *Saltwater Crossing*

It's never too late for a fresh start...especially on San Juan Island...

Tiffany Clifton knew that quitting her big city job and taking on small town life would be an adjustment. She was even prepared to work for her sister and confront just how far off-course her life had gone. What she was not at all ready for was having to verbally spar with a grumpy and ridiculously handsome developer Sidney on a regular basis.

Sidney Burke learned the hard way that romance isn't for him. So, he'd like nothing more than to avoid the lovely Tiffany. But if he wants to do business with her sister, that's not an option. He'll just have to somehow stay focused and ignore his inconvenient attraction to the woman who could so easily break down all the walls around his heart.

If Tiffany and Sidney want to take a shot at love, they have much to overcome...including the inconvenient secret that Tiffany's keeping. Will their foundation be strong enough to survive the trouble ahead—or will their happily ever after slip through the cracks?

Between this new romance and the murder trial for Morgan's mom, things only get more exciting in the fourth installment of the Westcott Bay series. Get your copy of *Saltwater Crossing* today and get lost in this sweet story of family, love, and starting over!

Would you like to join my reader group?

Sign up for my reader newsletter and get a free copy of my novella *Christmas at Saltwater Cove*. You can sign up by visiting: https://bit.ly/XmasSWC

About the Author

Amelia Addler writes always clean, always swoon-worthy romance stories and believes that everyone deserves their own happily ever after.

Her soulmate is a man who once spent five weeks driving her to work at 4AM after her car broke down (and he didn't complain, not even once). She is lucky enough to be married to that man and they live in Pittsburgh with their little yellow mutt. Visit her website at AmeliaAddler.com or drop her an email at amelia@AmeliaAddler.com.

Also by Amelia...

The Westcott Bay Series

Saltwater Cove

Saltwater Studios

Saltwater Secrets

Saltwater Crossing

Saltwater Falls

Saltwater Memories

Saltwater Promises

Christmas at Saltwater Cove

The Orcas Island Series

Sunset Cove

The Billionaire Date Series

Nurse's Date with a Billionaire

Doctor's Date with a Billionaire

Veterinarian's Date with a Billionaire